Cross-Country Crime

"Whoooee." Joe cut left, then right, then used some boulders on the ridge to his right to grab air. "Awesome!" he shouted as he lifted high above the slope. Grabbing onto his snowboard, he pulled a backside 360. For a moment, he was backward, facing the mountain. A second later, he'd spun frontward again and was ready to carve a landing square on the slope.

"Frank!" Joe yelled. "Check this out!"

Joe was about to find another rock and grab some more air when he heard a thundering sound behind him. He glanced over his shoulder in time to see a wall of white powder coming down the mountain. Spray flew, and big chunks of snow careened off the slope.

It was an avalanche—and it was headed straight for Joe!

The Hardy Boys Mystery Stories

Available from MINSTREL Books

THE **HARDY BOYS**® MYSTERY STORIES

134

CROSS-COUNTRY CRIME

FRANKLIN W. DIXON

A MINSTREL® BOOK

Published by POCKET BOOKS

New York   London   Toronto   Sydney   Tokyo   Singapore

This book is a work of fiction. Names, characters, places and incidents are products of the author's imagination or are used fictitiously. Any resemblance to actual events or locales or persons, living or dead, is entirely coincidental.

A MINSTREL PAPERBACK *Original*

A Minstrel Book published by
POCKET BOOKS, a division of Simon & Schuster Inc.
1230 Avenue of the Americas, New York, NY 10020

Front cover illustration by Brian Kotzky

Produced by Mega-Books, Inc.

ISBN: 0-671-50517-3

First Minstrel Books printing October 1995

10 9 8 7 6 5 4 3 2 1

THE HARDY BOYS MYSTERY STORIES is a trademark of Simon & Schuster Inc.

THE HARDY BOYS, A MINSTREL BOOK and colophon are registered trademarks of Simon & Schuster Inc.

Printed in the U.S.A.

Contents

CROSS-COUNTRY CRIME

1 Welcome to Evergreen

"Awesome!" Joe Hardy said, reaching the top of a mountain trail he and his brother, Frank, had been hiking since six o'clock that morning. "Civilization!"

Spread out below the Hardys was a crystal clear mountain lake bordered by another range of mountains that created a beautiful, snow-covered valley. The sun was rising over the tiny town of Evergreen, which was nestled in the valley right between the lake and the mountains.

"Down there somewhere is a hot meal," Joe said. "Eggs. Hash browns. Sausage. Not to mention hot chocolate."

"Well, let's not stand here talking about it," Frank said, readjusting the heavy backpack he was carrying. "Get a move on. We want to reach our next campsite before that storm comes in."

Since they had woken up that morning in camp, Frank had noticed clouds coming down from the north and west. It was only November, but unless Frank was wrong, they were going to get a lot of snow, and soon. Once they reached their next camp and pitched their tent, they could wait out the weather. Before that, hiking through a blizzard wouldn't be much fun.

Joe, seventeen, and his brother, a year older, had spent weeks arguing about where to spend their Thanksgiving break. Joe was promoting a nice, warm trip to Florida. "Why do you think they call it a break? 'Cause we all need a break from the cold," he pointed out to his brother. But Frank was looking for a challenge, and he convinced Joe they needed to toughen up. So now the Hardys were nearing the middle leg of a hard-core ski-hike vacation in the Rocky Mountains of Alberta, Canada. They'd arrived in the resort town of Banff three days earlier and had spent the entire time since then hiking and cross-country skiing through some of the most incredible wilderness they'd ever seen. The alpine lakes were sparkling blue and ice cold, and reflected the glaciers and towering mountains covered with the first heavy snowfall of the season. And up till that morning, the skies had been sunny and clear.

The Hardys had packed their snowshoes and their cross-country skis, and Joe had brought along a snowboard, too, hoping to get in some action. So far, there was the perfect amount of snow—just enough to get in some skiing, but not so much that the trails were hard-going. Snow camping was a lot of fun, and Frank, and even Joe, was having a blast.

When Joe had finally agreed to disappear into the wilderness for a week, Frank made sure there was a stop halfway to their destination. In Evergreen, they could load up on provisions and get a good meal for the road. The plan was to continue on to Lake Louise, where a bus would take them back to Banff—and their flight home to Bayport.

Frank and Joe had been hiking for half an hour, and a big breakfast sounded great. So great that Frank's stomach rumbled the whole way into Evergreen, as Joe tormented him with lists of his favorite foods.

"Roast beef sandwiches with Russian dressing," Joe said. "Blueberry pancakes, eggs, and bacon. Mom's French toast. Chow mein. Do you think we'll find some chow mein down here?"

"Doubtful," Frank said. "Isn't it a bit early for that anyway?"

Trekking through the town of Evergreen, Frank saw that it had a post office, a bank (or trust company, as Frank knew they were called in Canada), a convenience store, two ski rental shops, and a gas station, along with the private homes and ski condos that lined Main Street. There was also a café and a sheriff's station. On their way down Main Street, Joe spotted the Mount Summit Ski Resort nestled at the base of the mountain on their right. The resort had chairs, lifts, and a rental shop.

"We could get in some serious downhill," Joe remarked, pointing out the slope. "They've got some awesome vertical here."

"I'm more into cross-country this trip," Frank told him. "Besides, we've got all this gear, and there's a campsite up a ways that's got our names on it."

"Hard core to the end," Joe said proudly. "That's what I like about you, Frank. You don't mess around."

"I'm even more serious when it comes to a hot meal," Frank said, leading the way into the cozy café on the lake side of Main Street.

As soon as Frank and Joe walked inside, the room fell silent. A waitress behind the counter on their right smiled, while a half-dozen women and men sat at their booths and checked out the new faces in town.

The group kept staring as Frank and Joe walked the length of the café. "I guess they're not used to seeing strangers who get up as early as they do," Joe remarked under his breath.

"Especially the grungy kind," Frank added, running a hand through his dark brown hair. "Let's put our stuff down and wash up."

The waitress smiled as Frank and Joe sat down at the counter and took their jackets off. "How's it going?" she asked. "What can I get you boys?"

"How about a hot shower?" Joe joked.

"You look like you could use it." The young woman, who wore her blond hair in a ponytail, smiled again. "How's about some cocoa to start? And there's a rest room in the back."

"Thanks," Frank said. "We've been out in the woods."

The waitress took one look at their dirty jeans and rumpled flannel shirts and laughed. "I'd never have guessed," she said.

While Joe went back to wash up, Frank introduced himself to the waitress, whose name was Judy. By now, the other customers had gone back to their own conversations. Frank ordered breakfast for himself and Joe. When Joe came back, Frank headed for the rest room. Ten minutes later he returned to find Joe chatting with Judy and digging into his pancakes.

A thin man in his early forties wearing a sheriff's uniform came into the café and ordered a coffee to go. "You boys passing through?" he asked the Hardys, glancing at the heavy packs at their feet. When Frank nodded, he said, "Where you coming from?"

"Banff," Frank said, his mouth full. "We're on our way through the mountains up to Lake Louise."

"Camping?" the sheriff asked.

"You guessed it," Joe said.

The sheriff stared Frank down, narrowing his blue eyes on him. "Didn't happen to be here last night or early this morning, did you?"

"Nope," Frank said. "We were about two miles out last night, wouldn't you say, Joe?"

Joe shrugged. "I guess." He smiled. "My back sure feels like it."

"Hmmm," the sheriff said, examining their packs more closely. "Sheriff Hank Overton," he said, introducing himself.

"Frank and Joe Hardy," Frank replied.

"You mind if I look in your packs, Frank and Joe?" Overton asked. "I could try to get a warrant, but if you give me permission——"

Frank and Joe exchanged a look. "Go ahead," Joe said with a shrug.

The sheriff had already squatted down and unzipped the pack nearest to him. Frank knew that Joe had been the one to pack out their garbage the night before. He also knew the sheriff was headed right for it. He had no idea why Overton was looking through their things, but the man was about to get a big surprise.

"Phew!" the sheriff exclaimed, pushing the pack away from him and making a sour face. "You boys carrying around dead fish or something?"

"What goes in, comes out," Joe said, reciting an eco-friendly environmental saying. Frank noticed a twinkle in his brother's blue eyes.

6

The sheriff looked through Frank's pack for a few minutes. Once he was satisfied that Frank was carrying only camping supplies and clothes, he stood back up.

"Want to tell us what you're looking for?" Frank asked as he finished off his bacon.

"We had a robbery at the trust company here early this morning," the sheriff replied. "First one in twenty years."

Frank set down his cocoa, his instincts on alert. Back home in Bayport, Frank and Joe were known as crack detectives. News of a mystery always grabbed their attention.

"What happened?" Frank asked.

Overton shrugged. "The alarm sounded just after six. Six oh two to be precise. Whoever did it got away with fifty thousand dollars. We have reason to suspect that the thief escaped into the mountains."

"And you thought we had something to do with it?" Joe asked. "We're just a couple of happy campers."

Overton's smile was suddenly friendly. "I know that now, don't I? But until I looked in your pack, I had no way to tell." He paused. "Nope, I can see that you boys really have been out in the woods for days. I doubt you broke camp to head into Evergreen to rob a bank."

"We wouldn't have stayed for breakfast if we had," Frank said.

"Right you are." Overton paid for his coffee.

7

"Any witnesses to the robbery?" Joe asked.

"Maybe." Hank Overton smiled. "Why do you ask?"

"Just curious," Joe said.

"Well, Joe," Overton said, "stick around and you might find out more."

"No, thanks," Frank said. He flipped over the check and reached for his wallet. "Joe and I have a date with nature."

Overton left the café, and Frank and Joe did the same a few minutes later. Outside, the sky looked worse: dark gray and cloudy. The temperature seemed to have dropped, too. The Hardys stopped at the convenience store for provisions, dumped their garbage, and reloaded their packs.

"Maybe we *should* stick around," Joe suggested.

Frank knew his brother could never resist a mystery. Neither could he, for that matter, but this was one trip where he didn't want to get sidetracked by an investigation. He told his brother as much.

"Besides, look at this weather," Frank added.

"You're right," Joe agreed. "We're only halfway to Lake Louise, and there's a storm headed our way. We'd better get going."

Joe hoisted his pack onto his shoulder. Frank took out his Land and Forest Service maps and located the trail out of town. "It looks like we head southeast into the mountains, cut east through this valley here, then north into the pass."

Joe whistled. "Whatever you say, bro. I'm going to be looking for the snowboarding trails, so I'll count on you to keep us on track."

They walked down Main Street and turned right at First. Soon they were out of town, heading into the alpine forests. Snow-covered peaks towered above them. First Street petered out into gravel and then became an unpaved fire road. Everything was hushed, except for the noise they made as they hiked and the occasional sound of an animal in the woods. Twice already Frank and Joe had seen moose on the trail, and both Hardys knew that the bears had yet to enter their full winter hibernation. Nature was cool, but it could also be dangerous, so they kept their eyes and ears open.

After less than a mile, the snow started to come down. Ten minutes later, they were trudging through a full-fledged storm.

"This is bad," Joe said, his breath coming out as mist in the cold air. "You think we'll make it?"

Frank checked the map. "Five miles to camp," he said. "Keep yourself covered. It doesn't feel cold enough for hypothermia, but you never know."

The storm cut way down on their visibility. Pretty soon, they could only see ten feet or so in front of them. Frank made sure to keep an eye on the orange markers tied around the trees by the trail. The worst thing would be to get lost out in these woods. He'd planned ahead and packed a two-way radio and a first-aid kit, but the nearest help was way back in Evergreen.

"Hey, Frank," came Joe's voice, ahead of him on the trail. "Come here, quick!"

Frank climbed up a short hill to discover Joe tending to a man in the snow. The guy was unconscious. Next to him was a crashed snowmobile.

"He's coming around," Joe said. "But he looks bad."

Frank knelt down beside Joe. The fallen man, who appeared to be in his early thirties, had a red beard and thick red hair. There was a bad bump on his forehead, and his face was very pale.

Slowly the man blinked open his eyes. "Where am I?" he asked. "What happened?"

"You must have crashed your snowmobile," Joe said.

"Did I?" the man asked. He managed to sit up, then got a look at the wrecked machine. "I guess I did."

"Do you live around here?" Frank asked him.

The man held his head in his hand. "I—I don't know. Wait a minute." He closed his eyes and blinked several more times. "Yeah, I do. It's the weirdest thing," he said. "I know I live nearby, but I can't remember anything else."

"Amnesia," Frank said, recognizing the signs. "Do you know your name?"

"Sure," the man answered. "Mitch Taylor."

"We're Joe and Frank Hardy," Joe said. "We're

10

on our way to a campsite in the mountains. Can you stand up?"

The Hardys helped Mitch get up and take two wobbly steps. "I wish I could figure out how this happened," Mitch said.

"You hit your head in the crash," Frank said. "I've seen this kind of amnesia in skateboarding accidents," he added. "You remember some things but forget others. I'm sure you'll start to remember more in a few hours."

Mitch pushed back his long red hair. "I hope so. What if I've got a date, and I stand her up?"

Joe had to laugh. He liked a guy who could see the humor in a serious situation.

After making sure Mitch didn't have a concussion and performing some first aid on his head injury, Frank held him up and guided him up the trail, while Joe pushed the snowmobile alongside them. Mitch was able to remember the general location of his cabin, and more came back to him as they headed for his home. About a mile up the fire road, they came upon a clearing at the base of the mountain to the left. The cabin sat in the corner of the clearing, next to a sizable pile of firewood. The place was small and made out of logs; it had a wide porch that faced the mountain.

"Home sweet home," Mitch said. "You boys better come inside and wait out this storm. It's a good one. You won't make it to that campsite by nightfall."

11

Frank had a feeling that Mitch was right. It was only seven-thirty in the morning, and they had been hiking in the storm for about half an hour. The snow was getting heavier by the minute.

"Come on," Mitch said, urging them toward his house. "I'll make us something warm to drink, then you can help me try to figure out how I crashed my snowmobile up against that tree."

Joe shrugged. "May as well," he said to Frank. "No point in getting lost out here."

Frank had to agree. He followed Mitch and Joe inside, grateful to be out of the storm. Once they were indoors, Mitch made a fire in the cabin's big stone hearth. The Hardys settled in while Mitch washed up and changed his clothes. Outside, the snow accumulated even faster.

"It's really not letting up, is it?" Joe asked. "Do you think we'll be able to push on tomorrow?"

"Let's turn on the radio and listen to the news," Mitch said.

He stepped over to the bookshelves that lined the far wall of the living room. Next to the shelves was a TV, a stereo, and a CB radio. Mitch flicked on the AM/FM radio and tuned in to a news station. A weather report came on soon afterward. The news wasn't good.

"This Arctic front is here to stay for the next day or so," the announcer said. "Expect another one to two feet of accumulation."

"Rats," Joe said. [...]
trip?"

"I've never seen this mu[...]
said. "It's only November, a[...]
storm already."

Frank was thinking about how the [...]
get a ride to Lake Louise and forgo the [...]
trip—or at least wait out the storm in Ev[...]
when the local news came on.

"Reports from Evergreen indicate that the po[...]
there may have a lead in the robbery at the trus[...]
company that took place this morning. The thief
got away with fifty thousand dollars in cash. Sheriff
Overton says a witness has come forward and
identified a possible suspect. The witness has indicated that the suspect had long red hair and a red
beard, and that he disappeared from the scene on a
snowmobile. More news later on your all-news
station, WBNF."

Mitch's mouth dropped open in disbelief. He
turned off the radio, and the room fell silent. He
looked from Frank to Joe. They stared back at him.
Without saying a word, all three of them knew they
shared a single thought: Mitch Taylor was a prime
suspect in the robbery at the Evergreen Trust
Company.

"What about our camping
ch snow so early," Mitch
d this is the second
y might have to
rest of their
rgreen—
lice
t

What do you say when your host turns out to be a possible bank robber? Joe wondered. He glanced across the room at Frank, who looked extremely uncomfortable and more than a little worried.

"What are they talking about?" Mitch finally managed to say. "They think I robbed that bank, don't they?"

"They seem to have a witness who describes you accurately," Frank offered.

Joe remembered Frank's two-way radio. He couldn't signal his brother without tipping their hand, but Joe knew that the thing to do was find that radio, call Sheriff Overton, and get him out here to arrest Mitch. Fast. Before Mitch could do anything dangerous—like hurt them.

But Sheriff Overton had to know everyone within a hundred miles of Evergreen, Joe reasoned. That meant he also knew Mitch fit the description of the suspect. So chances were good that Overton was already on his way over to arrest Mitch.

"But I didn't do it," Mitch said, pacing the living room of his cabin. "I mean, not so far as I remember."

"You don't remember very much," Frank pointed out.

"Well, that's true, isn't it?" Mitch frowned. "You mean I might have done it, but then forgotten?"

Frank shifted uncomfortably. "I guess that's possible."

"But why would I have been stupid enough to rob a bank, right here in Evergreen, where the sheriff knows exactly who I am and where I live?" Mitch asked. The man was getting more and more agitated. He wrung his hands and pulled on his beard, all the while pacing like a caged animal.

Great, thought Joe. If Mitch was already hot under the collar, what would he do when the sheriff showed up? He and Frank had gone from being rescuers to potential hostages—in one short hour. Joe tilted his head toward the door. His message to Frank was unmistakable: Let's get out of here. Now.

Mitch abruptly stopped pacing and stood in the middle of the room, his eyes narrowed as he looked

15

first at Frank, then Joe. "You guys don't believe me, do you?" he stated with an edge to his voice.

Joe cleared his throat. The point was to keep Mitch calm, until they had a chance to beat it out of there. "We don't know what to believe, do we, Frank?"

"No," Frank agreed. He had moved toward the door, and Joe waited for a sign that Frank wanted to make a run for it too, storm or no storm. "Why don't you tell us what happened?" Frank asked Mitch, trying to calm him down.

Mitch scratched the top of his head. "Well, I wish I knew. I left my job at six A.M., when my shift ended. I work for the forest service in the national park on Mount Summit. That's outside town, on the south end. You kids probably came that way before you got to Evergreen."

When Frank nodded, Mitch went on. "I monitor the radio during the night, in case we get any kind of rescue calls. And I was doing some nighttime fire spotting before we got this snow."

"So you left at six," Joe put in. "Then what?"

"I got on my snowmobile to come home," Mitch said with a shrug.

"Which route did you take?" Frank asked.

"Through Evergreen," Mitch told them. "I cut south on First Street, like I always do, and onto the fire road where you found me. I must have crashed on my way home. That couldn't have been any later than six-fifteen or six-thirty. What time did you guys come along?"

Joe quickly calculated. "We left Evergreen about seven. So we must have found you no later than seven-thirty or so."

"I was out awhile," Mitch said. "No wonder I still feel so groggy." Then his dark brown eyes clouded over with worry. "What am I going to do?" he asked. "If they really think I robbed that bank, they'll be out to arrest me, you can count on that."

"My guess is, you're right," Frank said.

"I didn't do it!" Mitch insisted, this time with panic in his voice. He started pacing the floor again. "Man, oh man, you're in a real big mess this time, Taylor."

While Mitch paced and talked to himself, Joe realized that the guy wasn't a danger to him or Frank—at least for now. This was the perfect time for the Hardys to plan their strategy, before Mitch started to think about what they might do. Or what he should do to them.

"Mitch, I think my brother and I need to talk in private. Do you mind if we head outside?" Joe asked.

"Not at all," Mitch said. He waved toward the door. "Go ahead. Check out the snow. Walk off in the middle of the storm for all I care. Go back to Evergreen and bring back the sheriff. But I didn't rob that bank, and that's the truth."

Once they were out on Mitch's porch, staring at

the white face of the mountain just across the clearing, Frank let out a harsh laugh.

"We just can't seem to avoid a mystery, can we?" he said.

"Who wants to?" Joe asked.

"In this case, I'm not sure I want to get involved," Frank said.

"You mean because Mitch may not be innocent?" Joe asked.

"Exactly."

Mitch popped his head out the door. "You boys still here?" His worried expression dropped for a moment. "That's nice to know. The radio just reported that the storm seems to be pushing through. You'll have clear skies tomorrow, and a whole lot of fresh snow for skiing."

"Great," Joe said half-heartedly.

"Thought you'd like to know, in case the information changes your mind." With that, Mitch closed the door again and disappeared inside.

Frank shook his head. "He sure doesn't act like someone who's guilty. What should we do?"

"We can call Sheriff Overton on our radio," Joe suggested. "Or we can cruise out of town tomorrow morning and stay out of the whole thing. You heard Mitch—the sheriff knows where to find him. It doesn't seem like we're in any danger if we hang here for the night."

"I agree," Frank said. "If Mitch is worried that we're going to turn him in, he's not acting like it."

"Think of it this way," Joe said, holding the front door to Mitch's cabin open for his brother.

"What?" Frank asked.

"Neither of us has had a good night's sleep in three days."

"You know something? You're right." Frank gave his brother a serious look. "Let's just hope we don't regret this decision."

The next morning Joe was up at dawn, nervous and edgy to get going. He and Frank had spent the previous afternoon—and the evening—wondering when and if Sheriff Overton was going to show up. Occasionally, Mitch would turn on the radio to see if there were any news updates on the robbery. Several times he brought up the problem of how he was going to prove that he was innocent. But the Hardys stayed out of it. Mitch was a man with a problem, and Frank and Joe agreed before they drifted off to sleep that they weren't going to stick around Evergreen to help him out.

Joe shook his brother awake. Both Hardys were bunking in Mitch's living room on the two pull-out couches there. Joe slipped into the bathroom while Frank got dressed. By the time he came out, Frank was packed and ready to go.

"Check it out," Frank said, pointing to Mitch's dining-room table. "He made us lunch."

Joe went over to the table to find sandwiches, some fruit, and a note from Mitch. " 'Good luck on the trail,' " Joe read. He shook his head. "This guy is too good to be true."

"I was thinking the same thing," Frank said. While Joe grabbed the sandwiches and went to put them in his pack, Frank zipped up his backpack and rolled up his sleeping bag. Without looking up from his task, Frank said, "Maybe Mitch really is a good guy. Maybe we should stick around and help him out."

Joe gave his brother a surprised look. "But what about our plan?" he asked. "Three more days and we'll be in Lake Louise. Our flight leaves from Banff a day after that."

"I know, I know," Frank said. He made a face. "I just couldn't sleep too well last night, knowing we're about to bail on Mitch."

"You're assuming one thing," Joe said.

"What's that?" Frank asked.

"That he's innocent," Joe pointed out. "What if we stick around to help him, and the evidence starts stacking up against the guy?"

"True." Frank raised another point. "But we won't know that if we leave, will we?"

Joe sighed. Out the window of Mitch's cabin, the mountain was one long, wide slope of fresh snow. There was some great snowboarding out there, not to mention terrific skiing. Until they'd run into Mitch, he and Frank had been having a fantastic trip. But he had to admit that Frank was right. Even

20

Joe was bothered a bit about the thought of walking away from Mitch. Unless he was guilty.

"Listen," Joe told his brother. "We can talk to Mitch one more time before we leave. Since he's not up yet, why don't I head out into that fresh powder for a run on my snowboard? When I come back, we can figure out what to do about him."

Frank brightened. "Good idea. Let me grab my skis. I'll come with you."

Ten minutes later Frank was cutting through the valley behind Mitch's cabin on his skis, while Joe hiked up the slope carrying his snowboard in a specially designed backpack. He climbed high enough that Frank was a dot in the valley below and Mitch's cabin the size of a dollhouse. Smoke curled from Mitch's chimney, letting Joe know that the man was up and awake.

As he climbed, the altitude made it hard for Joe to breathe. But when he got to the top of the slope, it was all worth it.

"Intense," Joe said under his breath.

He could see over the next ridge and into the valley below. The sky was clear and blue with thin white clouds stretched across it.

Joe drew in a sharp breath and checked out the clean slope below him. He pulled the snowboard from his pack and strapped his feet into the bindings. He tested the bindings to make sure they were secure, and then, with a great big yell for his brother down below, Joe pushed off from the mountain.

"All right!" Joe cried.

The powder was perfect. It sprayed up around the board as Joe cut his turns wide and smooth. He bent his knees to keep his center of gravity low. Snowboarding was a lot like skateboarding but, in Joe's opinion, a whole lot more exhilarating.

"Whoooee." Joe cut left, then right, then used some boulders on the ridge to his right to grab air. "Awesome," he shouted as he lifted high above the slope. Grabbing onto his board, he pulled a backside 360. For a moment, he was backward, facing the mountain. A second later, he'd spun frontward again and was ready to carve a landing square on the slope.

"Frank!" Joe yelled. "Check this out!"

Joe was about to find another rock and grab some more air when he heard a thundering sound behind him. He glanced over his shoulder in time to see a wall of white powder coming down the mountain. Spray flew, and big chunks of snow careened off the slope.

It was an avalanche—and it was headed straight for Joe!

3 Attack of the Killer Logging Truck

"Joe!" Across the valley, Frank Hardy watched in horror as his brother was buried in a crush of snow. He seemed to vanish instantly before Frank's eyes. Even his colorful blue-and-green snowboard disappeared into the massive wall of white powder.

If Frank was going to save Joe's life, there wasn't much time. He whipped off his skis and went running through the knee-high snow toward the spot at the base of the mountain where he had last seen Joe. He was a hundred yards away when he spotted another man already there.

It was Mitch Taylor. He must have seen the avalanche from his cabin and raced to the spot. Now he was frantically digging with a shovel and calling out to Joe. Frank raced to his side and picked up the second shovel Mitch had brought over from the cabin.

"Help me out," Mitch said without pausing. "Look for his clothes," he added. "Just keep digging until you spot something that isn't white."

Snow was still tumbling down the mountain, but Frank could tell the worst was over. He moved about ten feet away from Mitch and started shoveling hard. The whole time a voice in his head said, He's alive. Keep digging.

Suddenly Mitch's voice broke Frank's concentration. "Frank!" he shouted. "Over here!"

Frank turned to the spot where Mitch was digging and saw a hand reaching from the snow. Next to the hand was Joe's brightly colored snowboard.

"Joe!" Frank cried. He stumbled toward the spot. Mitch was digging fast and hard. Together, they started shoveling the snow away with renewed determination. Joe's arm, and then his head, appeared.

"Wow," he gasped, his face flushed and red. "I wasn't sure how much longer my air would hold out."

Joe started to dig himself out with his hands. After another minute or so, Frank and Mitch had Joe pulled from the drift. He lay sprawled on his back, still gasping for oxygen.

"How you managed to stay conscious I'll never know," Mitch said. "That was some wall of white that came down on you."

Now that he was free, Joe could give in to some very real fear. He sat up and said breathlessly, "As soon as I saw that snow coming for me, I remembered reading that one way to survive an avalanche is to hold your board above your head. That way, the snow doesn't knock you out, and you create a gap of air to breathe."

"That was some fast thinking," Frank said, helping his brother to his feet and brushing off the snow that covered him from head to foot.

"Let's just hope I never have to use the information again," Joe said, shaking snow from his hair. "One near-death experience is enough for me, thanks very much."

Mitch put his arm under Joe's shoulder. Together, Mitch and Frank carted Joe back to the cabin and deposited him on the couch. Mitch fixed some hot tea to warm Joe up.

"You saved my life," Joe said to Mitch. "I could have been the new flavor of the month if it weren't for you."

Mitch smiled wearily. "I've tried to rescue more than one person from an avalanche before. Some of them don't make it. You were lucky, Joe."

"But you were there in a flash, Mitch," Frank said. "I doubt I could have run back to the cabin and grabbed those shovels in time to save Joe."

Mitch had turned on the radio. Now another announcement was on the news about the robbery in Evergreen. "The police predict an arrest will happen any day now. Sheriff Overton is quoted as saying that as soon as lab reports come in, he'll be taking appropriate action. In today's other news—"

"Maybe you can return the favor sometime," Mitch said absently, getting up to turn off the radio.

"Maybe we can," Joe said. And maybe we should, Joe thought. But he also couldn't help thinking that just because Mitch had saved his life didn't mean he wasn't the bank robber as well. There was only one way to find out. Joe glanced at his brother. "Are you thinking what I'm thinking?" he asked in a hushed voice.

"That we're not going to make it to Lake Louise?" Frank said with a smile.

"Mitch can always drive us back to Banff," Joe said. "We can't miss our flight home."

"No, we can't," Frank said. "But it sure does look like the rest of our trip is off."

"Why don't you tell him?" Joe said.

Frank nodded and began. "Mitch, there's something you should know about Joe and me. See, we're detectives and . . ."

An hour later, after the Hardys had offered to help Mitch and then gobbled down the huge breakfast he had fixed for them, they headed into town on Mitch's spare snowmobile. The day had turned clear and sunny, and even a bit mild for November. Joe had on a sweatshirt and a flannel jacket, and

26

Frank wore a windbreaker over a thick ski sweater. Businesses were just beginning to open for the day on Main Street, and there were actually a few cars on the road.

It wasn't hard to find the trust company. The two-story warehouse-style brick building sat at the corner of Main and First. Behind the bank, Joe could see the pristine blue waters of Lake Evergreen. The bank itself occupied the lower right-hand corner of the building. Next to the bank entrance was another entrance, and above that Joe saw a sign that read Ski Condos, Now Renting.

Sheriff Overton greeted them with a wave. "I see you boys decided to stick around." After giving a last order to a young officer by his side, Overton approached Frank and Joe. "What made you stay?"

"We promised Mitch Taylor we'd find out why he's a suspect in the robbery," Frank said.

The sheriff seemed surprised. "You did, did you? And how did you plan on doing that?"

"My brother and I are detectives," Joe told the man. "We've solved a crime or two in our day."

"And your crime-busting instincts tell you Mitch is innocent?" Overton asked, a smile at the corner of his mouth.

"Maybe." Frank drew out a notepad. "Why don't you tell us why you think he's guilty?"

Sheriff Overton held his hands out, palms up. "Whoa. Hold it there just a minute. Mitch Taylor is a prime suspect in my case, I'll admit it. But if you're here to prove he's innocent, then I can't—and won't—help you out. I may be backwoods, but I'm not stupid."

"We heard on the radio that you've got a witness," Joe said.

"Yes, I do," said the sheriff. "The boy who works at Mount Summit Ski Rentals across the street there claims he saw Mitch racing out of the alley here just after the alarm in the bank sounded."

Joe scanned the layout. Next to the Evergreen Trust Company was a narrow alley. Turning around, he saw that directly across Main Street, on the mountain side of town, was Mount Summit Ski Rentals. Whoever worked in that shop would have a bird's-eye view of what happened in the alley next to the bank, and of the building itself.

"So a witness says he saw Mitch coming out of the alley," Joe said. "That doesn't prove he was in the bank."

"When I get my report on the prints I found at the scene, I'll have the proof I need," the sheriff told him. "Then I'll be out to your friend Mitch's cabin, and it won't be a friendly call, you can be sure of that."

Joe narrowed his eyes in frustration. The sheriff seemed convinced that all the circumstances pointed to one thing: Mitch Taylor was guilty.

"What about security?" Frank asked. "Is there any videotape of the robbery?"

Overton smiled and shook his head. "This here's

a small-town bank, boys. We don't have that sort of technology. The door to the bank is wired to an alarm, and so is the vault. The alarm alerts the sheriff's station. We haven't needed anything more until now."

"Can we check out the bank ourselves?" Joe asked the sheriff.

"No way," Overton said, shaking his head. "I've got officers here from Calgary and Banff. You think I'm going to let them see me showing two kids around a crime scene?"

"I guess not," Frank said.

The Hardys were about to leave when a good-looking guy with thick brown hair and aviator sunglasses pulled up in a Jeep. He stopped the car to greet the sheriff. Joe judged him to be in his mid-forties.

"Hey there, Hank," the man said. "How's it going?"

"Fine, George, just fine," the sheriff called out.

"You any closer to solving this thing?" the man asked.

"Close to an arrest, sure," the sheriff said, nodding his head.

"So it *was* Mitch," the man replied, removing his sunglasses and peering intently at Overton.

Frank exchanged a look with his brother. Did everyone in town think Mitch was guilty?

"I guess I shouldn't be surprised," the guy said with a shrug. "I always thought Mitch was trouble.

29

That's why I fired him. This only proves I was right. Who are these kids?" he asked.

"Frank and Joe Hardy," Overton announced. "Meet George DuPuy. Frank and Joe are detectives." Frank wished the sheriff hadn't told DuPuy this information, but it was too late now.

"They seem to believe Mitch is innocent," Overton stated wryly.

"Oh, really?" DuPuy replied. His smile was wide and bright. "You kids obviously haven't been in town very long. Mitch Taylor has serious problems, and he's just made the list longer. Oh, well, see you around, Hank."

With that, the man pulled away. Once he was gone, Joe turned to the sheriff. "DuPuy will never join a Mitch Taylor fan club. What's he got against the guy?"

"Mitch used to work for George," the sheriff explained, "up at DuPuy Lumber, on Squaw Peak. Mitch tipped off some environmentalists about George's logging operations, and ever since George has had trouble with everyone. The Mounties, the Revenue Task Force, you name it. His business is practically ruined."

A red flag went up in Joe's mind. Were DuPuy's troubles bad enough for him to rob the trust company and try to frame Mitch? George sure did seem to have much more than a casual interest in the sheriff's plan to arrest Mitch.

"I've got to get back to work," Overton said. "But

before I do, I want you boys to promise me you're not going to make my life difficult around here. We both know the law says Mitch is innocent until proven guilty. But if the evidence stacks up against him, then I've got a case, and you can't stand in my way. You understand?"

"Sure," Joe said. "We wouldn't want it any other way. Right, Frank?"

"Right. We'll keep our promise as long as you promise us you won't tell anyone else we're investigating," Frank went on. "We like our anonymity."

"It's a deal. I'm glad we're agreed." Overton turned to head back into the bank. Once he was gone, Joe shared with Frank his theory about DuPuy.

"My thoughts exactly," Frank said, recording the information on his pad. "Let's find out where this DuPuy Lumber is. We need to ask George some questions."

"What about that witness?" Joe asked. "Should we head across the street to the ski shop first?"

"Sounds like a plan," Frank agreed.

Mount Summit Ski Rentals was on the mountain side of Main Street. The shop had racks outside for bikes, skis, and snowboards, and its front was painted in bright neon colors. In a large clearing behind the building, at the base of the mountain, Joe also spotted a helicopter, which he thought was strange until he remembered that skiers liked to use helicopters to take them to the backcountry.

The Hardys arrived at the front of the store to discover a note saying it wouldn't open that day until noon. Joe checked his watch to discover it was still only ten-thirty.

"Weird hours for a ski rental shop, wouldn't you say?" Joe asked aloud.

Frank looked around. "Maybe since the ski season hasn't officially started yet, they're opening later."

"But that witness claims he was working at six in the morning," Joe said. "And now the store isn't even open."

Frank shrugged. "Who knows? Let's ask directions to DuPuy's and come back down at noon."

The Hardys went back to the trust company to pick up Mitch's snowmobile. Frank asked directions to DuPuy Lumber from a police officer, and five minutes later Frank and Joe were cruising north out of town on a road that curved around the lake toward the Squaw Peak turnoff.

The road climbed into the mountains. Riding behind Frank on Mitch's snowmobile gave Joe the chance to take in the scenery. To their right, Squaw Peak rose to what Joe guessed must have been eight thousand feet. Its lower half was dotted with pine and spruce, but above the treeline the mountain was pure white.

Frank took the first turnoff. Soon they were heading to higher elevations. The road became narrower as it wound through the pine forest. After

32

a short time they reached a sign that read DuPuy Lumber, Private Property. Frank continued up the road, until they came to a big fence, swung open to reveal a wide clearing in the woods.

DuPuy Lumber consisted of five buildings, which were really nothing more than large trailers, a huge parking lot, and several logging trucks. There was also about a dozen very angry people holding signs and yelling.

"Stop clear cutting!" a young man with a beard yelled. Frank knew that clear cutting was a method of logging in which all the trees in a forest were cut down at once. It could devastate an ecosystem for years.

Protect our Environment, one sign read.

"DuPuy lies," a middle-aged woman shouted toward the main building of the lumberyard.

"Yikes," Joe said. "DuPuy really does have his hands full."

The protesters yelled at Frank and Joe as they drove on through the crowd. A few of them were even throwing eggs and rotten vegetables.

"Hurry," Joe urged his brother. He dodged an egg and heard it splatter behind him. "Last one there really is a rotten egg!"

Frank jammed through the crowd and pulled to a stop on the right side of the main trailer, just next to the lumberyard. There were several stacks of logs there and other bits of scrap wood.

"Let's keep some cover," Frank said, getting off the snowmobile.

"Good idea," Joe said. He looked into the trailer and saw DuPuy. The man got up from his desk, took what looked like a ledger book, and put it into a safe behind him. Then he shut the safe door and locked it with a key.

"Now, why would you keep a ledger book in your safe?" Joe asked. "Unless you absolutely didn't want someone else to see it."

By now Joe was practically leaning against the trailer. Frank stood behind him. Joe was vaguely aware of the sound of an engine close by. He assumed it was noise from the lumberyard.

"Frank?" Joe said, turning around. "Did you hear me?"

To get a better look inside the trailer, Frank had backed up onto the pile of uncut logs stacked a few feet away. He was leaning with his back against the pile when a logging truck pulled up just behind him. As Joe looked on, a set of giant metal claws rose from the truck.

"Frank," Joe said urgently.

There was an awful grinding of gears and metal as the claws descended on the pile of logs.

"Frank!" Joe said, louder.

But the noise of the gears drowned him out. Joe watched horrified as the claws went right for Frank.

4 Joe Gets Roughed Up

Frank heard an awful grinding sound behind him. He turned and found himself face-to-face with the biggest set of pincers he'd ever seen.

"Get down!" Joe cried out.

Frank ducked—and not a second too soon. The metal claws came down on top of the pile of logs behind him. Frank threw himself onto the ground and ate dirt. He craned his neck and watched as the claws closed in on three of the logs and raised them as if they were no heavier than twigs. Then the driver of the logging truck released the claws to deposit the logs onto the truck's huge bed.

Now was the time to make a run for it. Frank was just about to stand up and head for safety when the claws came grinding toward him—again.

"Watch what you're doing," Frank shouted to the driver, ducking down again. But the pile of logs was taller than Frank, and he was hidden behind them. Obviously, the driver couldn't see him.

Frank tried to back away from the truck, but he was trapped. The trailer was on one side of him, and the logging truck was on the other. His brother must have rushed out of the way when the truck first started loading the logs.

Frank saw Joe racing for the driver's door. He yanked it open and began to yell at the guy.

"There are people down here, buddy. What's your problem?" Joe shouted.

Frank was still staring down the heavy machinery. With a long screech, the monster claws stopped midmotion and hung just ten feet above him.

"Phew," Frank said in relief, once he was sure the machine had stopped. He ducked under it and headed over to where Joe was still chewing out the driver.

"Gosh, I'm sorry," the driver said. He was a young man, not much into his twenties. He had on a baseball cap, a red plaid flannel shirt, and blue jeans. When he saw Frank, he jumped from the cab and said, "Is this the guy?"

"You must not have seen me," Frank said.

The young man tugged at the bill of his baseball cap. "It's just that there are so many crazies around here these days. I'm supposed to have someone directing me when I use the rig, but everyone is busy. Really, man, I'm sorry." He reached out his hand. "Bill Forman. Who are you guys?"

"Joe and Frank Hardy," Joe said, shaking his hand.

"You're not with those nuts, are you?" Bill said, pointing to the environmentalists at the gate.

"No," Joe said. "We're here on our own."

"What for?" Bill wanted to know.

Frank stepped closer to the logging truck, hoping to keep out of sight of DuPuy's office. "We're friends of Mitch Taylor, actually," he told Bill.

"Really?" Bill's eyes moved from Frank to Joe. "Mitch sent you up here to talk to George about firing him?"

"Not exactly," Joe said.

Bill scowled in the direction of DuPuy's trailer. "Not that George would even listen to you guys. DuPuy's the coldest, meanest guy I've ever worked for. Talk about stingy." He gestured toward the group of protesters at the gate. "Personally, I'm glad Mitch turned George in. The guy deserves it. So how'd you get to know Mitch?"

"We're staying with him out at his cabin," Frank said. "We're trying to find out why everybody thinks he's guilty of robbing that bank yesterday."

"Is that what everybody's saying?" Forman asked, removing his baseball cap. A tumble of dark curls emerged. Forman pushed back his hair and said excitedly, "That's the biggest thing to happen

37

in Evergreen in probably a million years." Then he lowered his voice. "You don't think Mitch could have actually done it?"

"He says he didn't," Joe put in. "But he's got amnesia from a snowmobile accident and can't remember what happened."

Bill's eyes went wide. "Amnesia? That's intense. Is Mitch okay?"

Joe nodded. "It kind of makes it hard for him to prove he's innocent, though."

"You know," Bill said slowly, "I have a kind of wild theory, but tell me what you think. My bet is that George did it, and he's trying to frame Mitch."

"What makes you say that?" Frank asked, even though the idea lined up with some suspicions Frank and Joe had themselves.

"I've caught him talking on the phone a lot lately about how his ship is going to come in," Bill explained. "And I've seen him staring at those protesters and saying things like when he has the money for a lawyer he'll slap them all in jail. Now, where's he going to get the money for a lawyer? The guy's practically bankrupt so far as I can tell. Last month the payroll checks bounced—"

Just then the door to DuPuy's trailer popped open with such force it banged into the side of the trailer.

"Uh-oh," Bill said. He put his cap back on and turned to climb into the cab of his truck. "George must have seen that I've been shooting off my mouth when I should be working. Gotta go."

Bill hopped back inside the truck. Sure enough, DuPuy came out of the trailer, an angry expression in his eyes.

"What are you doing standing around, Forman?" he demanded. "You should have had those logs up and loaded by now."

DuPuy stopped yelling at Bill long enough to notice Frank and Joe, who were standing beside the truck.

"I know you guys. What're you doing here? You're not friends with this kid, are you?" DuPuy asked. "I told you I don't want your deadbeat snowboarding buddies hanging around," he barked at Bill.

"Go jump in a hole, George," Bill said.

With that, Bill slammed the door to the logging truck shut and began to operate the claw. The noise drowned out DuPuy. The owner of the lumber company shook his fist at Forman, then turned to the Hardys.

"Get off my property, you two." He pushed them toward Mitch's snowmobile. "And I don't want to see you back here. Got it?"

"Right," Frank said.

He and Joe piled onto the snowmobile. Frank started the motor, then gunned them out of the parking lot. As they passed by the protesters, the

Hardys heard more shouting and yelling. A man called out, "We saw what happened back there. You should file a complaint."

"I don't think so," Frank replied as they drove by. "But good luck!"

"That guy DuPuy sure is a creep," Joe leaned in to say to Frank, once they were heading back down the mountain. "He's a nasty boss—"

"And a crooked businessperson," Frank turned around to say.

"Not to mention just plain mean," Joe added.

"And he made such a nice first impression," Frank said sarcastically. For several minutes he concentrated on steering them back toward Evergreen. Once they had pulled up in front of the ski shop, Frank cut the engine on the snowmobile.

"Do you think DuPuy's financial troubles are bad enough to make him rob the bank?" Joe asked.

"Could be." Frank thought for a moment. "But even if George did rob it, we still don't know why this witness thinks Mitch did the job."

"I still say seeing Mitch drive down Main Street is a whole lot different than catching him with the bag of goods," Joe said.

Frank realized his brother had a point. "There's only one way to resolve this, and that's by going to the source. Come on."

Frank led the way to Mount Summit Ski Rentals. The helicopter was gone from the landing area in back of the rental shop. Inside, the shop's walls were plastered with posters of skiers and mountain bikers and, most of all, snowboarders.

"Cool, huh?" Joe asked his brother as they entered the store. "I smell the influence of some hard-core 'boarders in here."

The guy who came out from the back of the store had long blond hair and a goatee. He was wearing baggy pants, an oversize T-shirt, and funky, orange-shaded glasses.

"Word up?" he asked.

"Uh, we were looking for someone who works here," Frank said.

"You're looking at him," the guy said. "Except for the owner, I'm the only one who works here. How can I help you?"

"We came up here to do a little skiing," Joe said casually, "and we thought we'd check out your store. You were the guy who saw the bank being robbed yesterday, right?"

The boy had a worried expression on his face. "Well, yeah. Why do you ask?"

"I just think it's pretty wild, that's all," Joe said. He wanted to get the guy talking without having to admit he was investigating. "It's not every day you see something that exciting," he prompted.

"Yeah, it was," the boy said. "Unbelievable."

"We're Frank and Joe Hardy. I'm sorry, I didn't catch your name," Frank said.

41

"Justin," the boy said. "Justin Greeley." He reached out to shake their hands. "Pleased to meet you."

"What exactly did you see yesterday morning?" Frank prodded.

Justin seemed to like the attention and eagerly began to tell them his story. "I couldn't sleep. Since I live above the shop, I decided to come down and do inventory. That was about five forty-five. Just after six o'clock, I heard the alarm going off. I was about to call the police, when I saw Mitch coming out from around the trust company. He was on his snowmobile, and he came racing down Main Street."

"Did the police come?" Frank asked.

"Once the alarm went off, sure they did," Justin said. "But they were investigating at the bank so long that by the time they got to me, Mitch was long gone. I said they should head out and arrest Mitch, but Overton is waiting for more evidence, I guess. Tough luck for Mitch, though. Who would have guessed?"

Frank was about to ask another question when the door to the shop opened and a tall man who appeared to be in his late twenties and was wearing a distinctive red, green, and black ski suit walked in. "How's it going, Justin?" the man asked.

"Okay," Justin said. "Rob Rubel, meet Frank and Joe Hardy."

Rob nodded at the Hardys and went to look at a

rack of skis. He picked out a pair and brought them up to the counter.

"I'll take these," he said.

Frank recognized the brand Rob had picked out as one of the most expensive on the market. Justin reached for them and let out a low whistle.

"Wow, Rob," he said, holding them up. "How do you plan on paying for these?"

"Cold hard cash," Rob said. The smile on his deeply tanned face was broad and proud.

Rubel reached into his ski jacket, pulled out his wallet, and deposited five one-hundred-dollar bills on the counter.

"Where'd you get all that money?" Justin said with a laugh as he picked up the bills.

"Why do you ask?" Rubel countered suspiciously.

"If you keep flashing that much cash, people might jump to the wrong conclusion."

"Such as?" Rob asked, glancing at Frank and Joe.

"Such as maybe *you* were the one who robbed the Evergreen Trust Company," Joe joked.

"That's not very funny," Rob said. He wasn't smiling.

Joe realized that Rob didn't have much of a sense of humor. "Sorry, man," he said, backing off. "Didn't mean to get you upset."

But Rob wasn't going to accept Joe's apology. "Well, you did," he said, advancing on Joe. His arms were stiff at his sides, and his expression grew angrier by the second. "I don't like your implication, or your manners."

"I said I was sorry," Joe said.

"I didn't hear you," Rob said. He came closer to Joe and grabbed him by the shirt collar. "Say it louder, Joe, before I punch out your lights."

5 Collision Course

"It was a joke!" Joe Hardy sputtered. He was only an inch away from the nasty expression in Rob Rubel's cold blue eyes. "I said I was sorry."

Rubel shoved Joe away from him. "I don't have a sense of humor about that sort of thing, Joe." He turned to Justin. "That money's mine, fair and square," he said. "Give me my change so I can get out of here."

"What about bindings?" Justin asked.

"I'll mount them myself," Rubel said. "Next time I'm in here, Justin, be sure to watch what you say."

"Sorry, Rob," Justin mumbled. As soon as Rubel left, Justin let out a long sigh. "Sheesh," he said. "Someone sure did wake up on the wrong side of the bed this morning."

"I admit it wasn't a very funny joke," Joe grumbled, "but he didn't have to get so upset about it."

Justin closed the drawer of the cash register and shook his head slowly. "If I didn't know better, I'd wonder if maybe he *did* have something to do with that robbery."

"I thought you saw Mitch leaving the bank," Frank said.

"Well, yeah, sure I did," Justin said. "But maybe Rob's working with Mitch." He shrugged. "All I can tell you is that I've been selling skis and other stuff to Rob since he first started coming to Mount Summit, and he's never had the money to pay for anything that expensive. In cash!"

"Maybe we should check out Rubel," Frank suggested to Joe. "Didn't you say you wanted to get in some downhill action anyway?"

"You bet," Joe said with excitement. He remembered the lifts he'd seen all up and down the mountain the day before, when he and Frank had come into town. "We can get in a few runs, check out Rob, and head back to Mitch's before it gets dark."

Justin rented Frank and Joe each a set of downhill skis, boots, and poles. He adjusted the bindings on the skis and directed them back behind the shop where they'd find an entrance to the resort.

"The parking gate is on Main Street," Justin explained. "But there's a trail up to the main entrance that goes by the base of the mountain."

Joe balanced their gear while Frank drove the snowmobile up to Mount Summit Ski Resort. They found a place to park the snowmobile and a locker to stow their shoes in. After eating a quick lunch in the cafeteria, Frank and Joe rode the main lift up the mountain.

"How are we going to find Rob?" Joe asked, turning in the chair to check out the slopes. "It looks like there are at least ten runs, and they're spread out all across the mountain."

Frank had a map unfolded on his lap. He held it with one hand, while he gripped his poles with the other. "There are only two expert slopes," he said. "Headwall and Charley Horse. Rob is sure to be on one of them. Ready for some hard-core action?"

Joe smiled, feeling his heart beat quicker with anticipation. "You mean tracking down Rob, or taking my first expert run this year?"

"Both."

The lift came to the top of the mountain, and Frank got ready to hop off. Joe jumped beside him, only Frank planted his pole right in the middle of Joe's skis. As Joe pushed off from the chair, the pole prevented him from going any farther, and he fell on his backside into the slush.

Frank cruised on off the lift, leaving Joe in a heap. A chair attendant stopped the lift and came over to help the younger Hardy, who was cold and wet from the fall—and peeved.

"Thanks, bro," Joe said. "You tripped me with your pole!"

"I did not," Frank insisted. "You didn't stay on your side."

"Next time, don't ski into me, okay?" Joe stuck his hands through his pole grips.

"Next time, watch your step," Frank replied. "You always fall off the lift the first time."

"That's because you don't know what you're doing," Joe shot back. "Which way to Headwall?"

Frank pointed to another lift several yards away that went straight up the mountain to their right. The white peak climbed into the sky. It looked as if the slope itself was almost a pure ninety-degree drop.

"No wonder they call it Headwall," Joe said, taking in a deep breath. "If you wipe out on that hill it's like ramming your head into a wall."

"There's a café at the top," Frank said. "I guess some people take the lift just to check out the view."

"Or maybe once they get there, it's too scary to head down."

Joe led the way to the lift up Headwall. This ride was a bit hairier, and he had to force himself to look up and not down. To his right, Frank pointed out a familiar figure, dashing down the slope in perfect arcs.

"There he is," Frank said. "There's Rob."

Joe caught sight of Rob's telltale red, green, and

black ski suit. His form was pretty incredible. Fresh powder sprayed up from his skis with each turn. Rubel kept his weight low and forward, and even from the lift Joe could tell he had good speed.

"So we catch up to him, and then what?" Joe asked his brother, turning his eyes back to the mountain in front of them.

"Tail him. Ask around. See if anyone else has seen Rubel spreading out the cash," Frank said. "Maybe we can find out who his friends are and question them privately about him."

"Let's make sure he doesn't spot us," Joe warned. "I doubt Rob would be happy to know we're spying on him."

"Right," Frank agreed. He pointed in front of them. "We're coming to the end here, Joe," he said. "Be careful and don't ski too close to me."

"Thanks for the tip," Joe said, getting ready. "Just keep your poles to yourself this time."

Joe and Frank managed the lift this time without either of them falling, then skied over to the top of the trail. Skiers dotted the run in their colorful outfits. From what Joe could tell from watching them take the run, the first series of turns seemed smooth and easy; the skiers were taking them at a clip. But just below the third turn, Joe saw that the trail dropped off steeply. He couldn't even see the slope again until midcourse, where groups of skiers stood off to the side, taking a break after some rough moves.

"Here goes nothing," Frank said, adjusting his goggles. "See you at the bottom."

Joe shoved off right after his brother. Together, the Hardys schussed down the first part of the slope. Joe was having the time of his life—until he came to the steep part of the mountain.

Maybe it was the skis, maybe the slope, but Joe's tips crossed at the first mogul he encountered, and he lost his balance. He put his poles out, but it didn't help. He went sprawling across the snow face first and didn't come to a stop until he was practically in the trees.

From where he sat, Joe saw Frank cruise on ahead, planting his poles hard for balance and cutting the turns as if they were nothing.

"Nice moves, bro," Joe said. "See you at the bottom—eventually."

Joe used his poles to pull himself up and brushed the snow off his body. He let two skiers ski by, then pushed off. This time Joe stuck to the parts of the slope that seemed less steep. Cutting his turns wide, he made sure not to pick up too much speed. A few curves later, Joe found his rhythm. By the time he got to the bottom, he was cruising hard. Frank was waiting for him at the lift. Joe came to a stop with a spray of snow.

"About time," Frank said.

"That was fun," Joe said. "Once I got warmed up."

"That spill must have cooled you right off,"

Frank joked. "Maybe you should stick to snow-boarding."

"Very funny," Joe said. "Maybe you should stick to detective work."

"I have." Frank told Joe he'd seen Rob Rubel. "He went back up the mountain. He had some friends with him, too, and I heard him say they were heading for the café to grab some lunch."

"So? What are we waiting for?" Joe asked.

Ten minutes later Frank and Joe were scanning the café at the top of the mountain. "There he is," Joe whispered, pointing Rob out to Frank.

At a cash register ten feet from where Frank and Joe were standing, Rob Rubel was surrounded by about five people, all of whom had the tanned good looks of ski bums. Rubel peeled a half-dozen bills from his wallet.

"Check it out," a guy next to Rob shouted. "Rubel's paying!"

"Haven't you heard?" another one asked. "Rob's struck it rich. New skis, lunch for everyone. He's even going to pay his rent on time this month."

Rob punched the guy lightly on the arm. "Cut it out, Dan," he said. "Or I might change my mind and let you pay for your own burger and fries."

Frank and Joe hung back as Rubel and his buddies entered the dining room with their trays. "How about that?" Joe asked his brother. "Rob's flashing the cash again."

Frank nodded. "We need to ask around town,

find out where else Rob might have come by that money. If we can't find any answers, then I'd say we've got another suspect to look at."

Joe thought for a moment. "There's just one problem. If you robbed a bank one day, would you let people see you spending the money the next day?"

"I wouldn't, but maybe Rob's just plain stupid." Frank narrowed his eyes on Rob and his friends. "Or maybe he figures the best way to hide a haul is right out in the open. Let's keep our eyes on him and stay low. We still don't want him to think we're after him."

For the next several hours Frank and Joe skied Headwall, and then moved over to Charley Horse when Rob took on that trail. After a half-dozen runs, the Hardys were cold, hungry, and tired. They decided they weren't going to learn much more from tailing Rob. The brothers took the lift back down and headed to Mount Summit Ski Rentals to turn in their gear. After that, they headed down First Street and onto the fire road that led back to Mitch's.

Joe was steering the snowmobile, and Frank was riding behind him. About a mile out of town, near the spot where the Hardys had first seen Mitch, Joe caught the sound of another snowmobile in the woods.

"Hear that?" he asked Frank.

"Slow down," Frank urged. "We might run into someone else on the trail."

Joe cut the power. The sound was coming from the woods on his left. But as far as he remembered, there was only one road out here, and that went straight toward Mitch's cabin.

"It's too high-pitched to be a snowmobile," Frank said. "That sounds more like a chain saw."

Joe figured his brother must be right. "I guess someone's cutting wood." He notched the power up again. "No need to slow down if it's not someone on the trail," he said, speeding ahead.

The sound kept getting louder. Joe steered the snowmobile through a wooded stretch and into a clearing. From a distance he caught sight of another, smaller path that entered the main trail from his left.

"I wonder if that's where the sound's coming from," Joe said.

A second later he had his answer. Joe was just about to enter the spot where the two trails met, when a figure came flying out of the path.

"Watch out!" Joe cried.

But it was too late. The Hardys were on a collision course with the guy, and there was no stopping him.

6 Hot Doggy Dog!

At the last possible moment, Joe Hardy swerved out of the path of the incoming snowboarder, shouting "Watch where you're going!" as he passed.

Joe turned so hard that Frank went flying off the back of their snowmobile. He landed in a heap in the snow. The 'boarder crashed into the trees on the other side of the trail. And Joe came to a hard stop up ahead, only inches from the trunk of a pine tree.

"Where'd you guys come from?" the 'boarder demanded, sitting up in the snow. "There's never anyone on this trail."

"And that gives you an excuse to go a million miles an hour on that thing?" Frank shot back.

Joe came cruising back to where they were to

make sure Frank and the boy were okay. Frank pulled himself up and took a long look at the boy's contraption, which was lying in the snow beside him. It looked like a snowboard, but it had an engine on the back and a thick-tread tire attached to it. There was also a long stick the boy had been using to steer the snowboard.

"What is that thing anyway?" Frank asked.

"It's a motorized snowboard," the boy said.

"Wow," Joe said. "Cool."

The boy stood up and brushed the snow off the long, bright blue plaid jacket he wore. "Thanks. Sorry I almost beaned you guys."

Frank's frown lightened. "I guess it wasn't really your fault. Sorry I got so heated up."

"Now that you two are friends," Joe said, "do you want to explain that contraption to me?"

"My dad helped me build it," the boy said. "My regular snowboard slides onto the platform. I use an old lawn-mower engine to power it and a fat tire to keep me going. Want to try?"

"You bet," Joe said.

The boy happily handed over his board to Joe. "By the way, my name's Tom Gregory, but all my friends call me Hot Doggy Dog."

"Hot Doggy Dog?" Frank repeated.

Tom smiled. He had a gap between his front teeth, and with his red hair and freckles, he looked as if he were about twelve.

"It's 'cause I'm so good on the board," Tom explained.

While Joe tried out Tom's board, Frank learned more about the guy. It turned out that Tom was coming home on the trail from Secret Valley. "It's a totally hot snowboarding spot," Tom explained. "Do you 'board?"

Frank shook his head. "I'm strictly downhill and cross-country. But I'm into learning. It looks like a lot of fun."

"No question." Tom watched Joe spin out on the trail. "I use the motor on the board to get me back and forth from Secret Valley. It's easier than walking, that's for sure." He glanced at the snowmobile. "And it doesn't destroy the trail like one of those."

"I get your point," Frank said.

"So what brings you guys to beautiful, boring Evergreen, the dullest town in the West?" Tom asked.

Frank laughed. "I don't know what you mean. We've had an exciting time so far." Then he explained how they'd found Mitch the day before, and heard that Mitch was a suspect in the robbery. "Joe and I decided to stick around to see if we could help Mitch, especially after Mitch more or less saved Joe's life in an avalanche—"

"Hold it right there." Tom's blue eyes lit up in surprise. "You guys have had more happen to you in one day than I've had happen to me in a whole twelve years."

"Maybe you need to get out more," Frank joked. "Anyway, Joe and I feel kind of obligated to find out what we can about the robbery."

Tom crossed his arms and stuck his hands under them to keep them warm. "I heard about that robbery. If you guys think Mitch didn't do it, then you're probably the only ones. How're you going to prove it?"

"It'll be hard," Frank agreed. "Mitch lost his memory when he crashed his snowmobile. We're hoping he'll get some memory back. Otherwise, we're on our own."

"This thing is a real blast," Joe said, roaring up on Tom's snowboard. "I'm just mad that I didn't think of it first. Why don't you come on up to Mitch's cabin with us? That way I can ride this some more."

"You think Mitch would mind?" Tom asked.

"I don't see why," Frank said. "You know, maybe it's a good idea to have Tom help out. He knows the town and the people. He could give us some tips."

"Are you up for that?" Joe asked.

Tom grinned. "Are you kidding? I'm so bored in this town I could scream. Let's book."

Frank and Tom piled onto Mitch's snowmobile. With a whoop, Joe gunned Tom's board past them and led them up the trail, cutting wide turns through the snow all the way.

When they got to the cabin, Mitch was shoveling

snow off the porch. He didn't seem very happy to see someone with Frank and Joe.

"What's with the kid?" he asked Frank after Tom and Joe had gone inside.

"He's Tom Gregory," Frank said. "Otherwise known as Hot Doggy Dog."

"I know who he is. What's he doing here?" Mitch asked, confused.

"We asked him to come along," Frank explained. "I thought it might help to have someone working with us, someone who knows the town."

"*I* know the town," Mitch protested.

"But you're a suspect," Frank reminded him. "You can't go snooping around town for information."

Mitch's eyes dropped, and his expression turned glum. He ran his hands through his beard and said, "I guess you're right. I can't help you much, especially hiding out here, waiting for Overton to come out and arrest me. And everyone else in town thinks I'm guilty, too."

"We're going to get to the bottom of this," Frank assured him.

Mitch sighed. "I hope you're right. I sure hope you're right." With that, Mitch yanked open the front door and stepped inside. "Who's for hot chocolate?" Frank heard him call out.

Frank stood on the porch a moment longer. The snowmobile Mitch had crashed in his accident lay in the front clearing. Frank wondered if Mitch was planning to work on it, or if he was going to turn it into scrap. Right now, Mitch was probably having a hard time making any kind of decision. It couldn't be easy to wait around and see if you were going to be arrested and locked up in a cell.

Inside, Tom and Joe were drinking some hot chocolate at the dining-room table while Mitch built a fire in the living room. Mitch had invited Tom to stay for dinner, and he'd called his house to let his parents know that he'd be home later. Frank joined his brother and Tom at the table.

"Here's what we know so far," Frank said. "Thanks to you, Mitch, George DuPuy has trouble up at his mill, and is in financial difficulties because of it."

"You didn't waste any time," Mitch said. He was at the kitchen counter, shredding cheese. "I only reported what everyone already knew about his logging operation. It's not my fault that George has problems because of it."

"No, it's not," Joe agreed. "But he could hold a grudge against you."

"You think George DuPuy robbed the trust company?" Tom asked, sipping his hot chocolate.

"Maybe." Frank told Tom and Mitch what Bill Forman had said—that DuPuy did it and was framing Mitch.

Tom scowled. "I wouldn't believe a thing Bill said. He's a 'boarding buddy of mine, but he sure does like to stretch the truth."

Frank made a note of Tom's observation. Then he went on. "We also checked out Rob Rubel. The guy bought a brand-new pair of really expensive skis, just this morning."

"And then he went and bought lunch for all his friends," Joe added. "It had to be easily a five-hundred-dollar day for the guy, and Justin Greeley says last winter he was an ordinary ski bum with no spare change. So what happened?"

"Rob's a real possibility," Tom said. He leaned forward in his chair and drummed his fingers on the table. "I've heard he's got a record."

Frank's ears pricked up at the information. "That gives us two solid leads. First of all, we need to learn more about DuPuy's financial problems. Second, we should find out what we can about Rob's record. I'll put in a call to Con first thing tomorrow morning."

"Who's Con?" Tom asked.

Joe realized he might have said too much. He hadn't wanted to reveal his detective status to Tom, but the boy seemed trustworthy. "Con Riley. He's our contact at the Bayport Police Department back home," Joe explained. "He helps us out when we're investigating a case. Like now."

"Investigating? A case?" Tom repeated. "Are you guys, like, detectives or something?"

"You got it," Joe said. "But you've got to keep that to yourself. Think you can handle it?"

"No problema," Tom said. "You can trust me."

60

Mitch came out of the kitchen and into the dining room. He stood rubbing his beard and said, "I appreciate what you kids did today. You believe in me, and that really counts. Thanks."

"Don't mention it," Joe said. "Frank and I live for a mystery, and now that we know Tom, we're going to check out the local snowboarding action. Call it a working vacation."

"I just wish I could remember what happened that morning!" Mitch exclaimed. "But every time I try, my mind is still a great big blank."

Frank thought for a moment. "I remember reading somewhere that amnesia victims sometimes regain their memory—that it can be jarred if they reenact the series of events that caused the memory loss."

"You mean have Mitch reenact the morning of the bank robbery?" Joe asked.

"Yeah," Frank said. He chewed on his lower lip in concentration. "We could start from the moment that he left work. Then follow the route he took when he rode through town. Right up to the point where he crashed. Something could jar loose, something he remembers just because he's going through the same series of events at the same time."

Mitch scratched his beard. "It's an idea—" He was about to go on, when there was a knock at the door. "Mitch, it's Hank Overton. Open up, would you?"

The room fell silent. Everyone knew why Sheriff Overton had arrived, and no one was happy about it. Mitch took a deep breath, walked through the living room, and opened the front door.

"Hi, Hank," he said. "You here on business or pleasure?"

Frank could see Overton peeking inside Mitch's cabin. "I think you know, Mitch. You were seen at the trust company around the time of the robbery, and we have some fingerprints we'd like to check against yours. I'm going to have to take you in."

While Overton put Mitch in cuffs, Frank, Joe, and Tom went to the front door. Poor Mitch! Frank really felt for the guy.

"We've got to do something," he whispered to Joe as Hank Overton led Mitch to a waiting Jeep. There was a deputy with him, and Mitch nodded hello to the man.

"Like what?" Joe asked.

"Like solve this crime," Frank said. "What do you think?"

"Sorry, boys," Mitch said, giving them all a last look. "The chili's on the stove, and you can stay as long as you need to. Take care of the place for me, okay?"

"Sure," Frank said. "We'll visit you tomorrow, all right?"

The sun was just setting through the pine trees as Mitch rode off in the back of the sheriff's Jeep.

Frank, Joe, and Tom waited until Mitch, the sheriff, and his deputy were out of sight.

"Wow," Tom said softly. "That was weird. They took him away, just like that."

Frank drew in a sharp breath. Until tomorrow, there wasn't much more they could do. Except . . . "You know, we never did go over the snowmobile for clues," Frank observed.

"You're right," Joe said.

Tom was puzzled. "I don't get it. What kind of clues would we find in a snowmobile?" He laughed. "Especially that snowmobile. If you want proof that it was in an accident, all you have to do is look at the thing."

"We need some clues about what happened *before* Mitch's accident," Frank explained. "And before the accident, he was on the snowmobile. You never know what you'll learn when you look for clues."

He led the way to the clearing in front of the porch. Mitch's snowmobile lay in the same spot where Joe had dragged it the day before. From a distance, there wasn't any sign that Mitch had even touched it. But when Frank got closer, he noticed that the rear panel was partially removed.

"Wonder what Mitch stored back here," Frank said to his brother.

Joe shrugged. "Let's check it out."

Frank found that the panel was still attached

with two screws. He dug out his pocketknife and used it to unfasten the panel the rest of the way. When he did, it popped off, revealing a tool kit underneath.

There wasn't anything else in the compartment, so Frank opened the tool kit. But he didn't find any tools. Instead the kit was filled with five stacks of neatly wrapped twenty-dollar bills.

"Wow," Tom said. "Where'd Mitch get all that money?"

Frank and Joe looked at the money, and then each other. "I know the most obvious answer," Frank said.

"What's that?" Tom asked.

Joe let out a long sigh. "Evergreen Trust Company," he said. "I guess we have to face the facts, Frank. It's very possible that Mitch really *did* rob that bank."

7 Eight-by-Ten Dorks

"No way!" Tom's eyes grew even wider. "Mitch says he didn't rob the bank."

"So how did he get all this cash?" Frank Hardy asked.

"That's what I want to know," Joe said. "But I'll bet you anything Mitch would claim he didn't know about this money. In fact, I wonder if Mitch has been snowing us this whole time."

"There's just one problem with that theory," Frank said. "If Mitch did know about this money and stashed it here, why didn't he move it when he had the chance? We were gone all day. There's got to be better hiding places around here. I think this looks like a frame."

"And I'm telling you we're the ones who've been

framed—into eight-by-ten pictures of dorks!" Joe kicked at the snowmobile and felt a stinging pain as his toe made contact. "Ouch. That hurt."

"Take it easy," Frank said.

"I'm going to," Joe said. He felt his anger rising even more at the thought of what they'd done for Mitch. "I'm going to ease right on out of here and finish my vacation."

Tom still seemed perplexed by this latest turn. "I think Frank's got a point, Joe. Why would Mitch want you to stick around if he really did rob that bank? You'd only find out he was guilty. No, it doesn't make sense. I think someone planted that money so we'd all suspect Mitch."

"In that case, we're under more pressure than ever," Frank said. "We've got to find out who really did rob the trust company, before the sheriff goes ahead and railroads Mitch."

Joe scowled. "I guess you're right. But what are we going to do about this money? We have to tell the sheriff, right?"

"You bet we do," Frank said. "We can't conceal evidence."

Frank bent down to get a closer look at the stash of bills. "It looks as if they're all twenties," he said, fanning a stack to check.

"Wow!" Tom said. "I've never seen fifty thousand dollars in my whole life."

"Hate to disappoint you, Tom, but I don't think

you're looking at anywhere near that much," Frank said.

"What do you mean?" Joe asked.

"It looks more like five thousand to me," Frank said. "Take a look."

"I think you're right," Joe said. "So where's the other forty-five thousand?"

Frank and Joe looked at each other and said nothing. Tom ended the silence by saying, "Let's start searching! Maybe it's buried in the snow or in a tree trunk."

But neither Hardy was terribly eager to begin hunting for the money in the cold, dark forest.

"This money means one of two things," Frank said. "Either the crooks didn't want to part with their money and left just five thousand here to frame Mitch . . ."

"Or?" Tom said curiously.

"Or," Joe began, standing up, "Mitch has the rest of it stashed somewhere else and didn't finish hiding it before we came back."

"This is, like, totally mysterious," Tom said. "Real money and everything."

Frank headed inside the cabin to call Sheriff Overton, while Joe and Tom put the chili in bowls. Half an hour later, the sheriff arrived with his deputy.

"Looking bad for Mitch," Overton said after he saw the cash hidden in Mitch's snowmobile. "You kids should just go on home. There's no mystery here. He's guilty."

The Hardys and Tom watched in silence as Overton and his deputy hitched Mitch's snowmobile up to a tow rope and dragged it away as evidence. After the sheriff was gone, Tom got ready to leave.

"You guys want me to show you around Secret Valley tomorrow morning?" Tom asked. "We can get in some runs before you go into town."

"Sounds good," Frank said. "I'll call Con first thing, and then we can head out with you. If we get an early start, we'll still have the whole day to investigate Rubel and DuPuy."

The Hardys said goodbye to Tom, cleaned up the dishes, and got ready for bed. It had been a long day, and Joe was wiped.

"You really think Mitch is innocent," he said to his brother as he unrolled his sleeping bag.

"I do," Frank said. "I think someone planted that money in his snowmobile, and when we find out who did it, we'll also know who robbed that bank."

Joe yawned. "I hope you're right, bro." He unzipped his sleeping bag and crawled into it. "I hope you're right."

The next morning Frank was up at six. While Joe was still asleep, he fished the two-way radio out of his pack and turned it on. Soon he had Con Riley on the line. Because of the time difference, Con was at his desk. Frank quickly explained why he was calling.

"R-u-b-e-l," Con said. "Got it. I'll run a search and get in touch with you as soon as I find out something."

"Thanks, Con," Frank said. "Over and out."

On the couch across from him, Joe was just stretching awake. "What's for breakfast?" he asked.

"Whatever you make for yourself," Frank said. "Who do you think I am, Mitch?"

In the next hour Frank and Joe got dressed and had a quick breakfast of cereal and milk. Tom came knocking at seven.

"You guys ready?" Hot Doggy Dog called out. "Conditions are prime!"

Frank opened the door to Mitch's cabin to find a smiling Tom Gregory, dressed in his familiar bright blue coat, carrying a pack on his back and a spare snowboard in his hand.

"Where's the motor?" Frank asked, taking the board that Tom handed him.

"I only have mine," Tom apologized. "But I can get my dad to make you guys one if you want. He's put them together for all the guys who 'board out in Secret Valley."

Frank laughed. "I wouldn't want to be left out."

"Get a move on, Joe," Tom called past Frank. "What's taking him so long?"

"I'm ready, I'm ready." Joe Hardy came to the

front door and pulled it shut. "I had to find all my gear."

Frank took one look at his brother and had to laugh. Joe was wearing every piece of ski gear he'd brought along, and all at once. He had on a black ski cap, wraparound sunglasses, baggy pants, and an orange long-sleeve T-shirt underneath a thick flannel coat like Tom's, only in bright green.

"Quite the fashion statement," Frank said to his brother. He pointed to his own clothes. "What's wrong with jeans and a sweater?"

"Nothing." Tom checked out Frank's outfit. "Except you might get cold and wet."

Frank shrugged. It didn't seem to him that Joe's wild getup was going to prevent him from getting wet, but he didn't say anything.

Tom jumped off the porch with a loud yell. "Awwwriight!" he cried. "Let's do it!"

The three boys headed onto the fire road that led into Evergreen. When they came to the turnoff where they'd run into him the day before, Tom took them onto the side trail. Soon they were hiking deep into a desolate, narrow canyon. On either side, the walls grew steeper and the terrain was rougher. Overhead, Frank heard the sound of a helicopter. He remembered the copter he'd seen by Mount Summit Ski Rentals and asked Tom if he thought that was it.

"Could be." Tom looked overhead. "Len Grossman, the guy who owns the rental shop, runs flights up to the top of Mount Summit. He drops skiers off there. The snow's incredible, and it's a great ride down. But when it's slow, Len also lets Justin use the copter to take the guys out to Secret Valley."

The canyon trail grew steeper, and the three began breathing so hard that they couldn't keep up the conversation. After they'd hiked awhile longer, they came to a rise. The trail opened out, giving them a clear view of the valley below.

"There it is," Tom said. "Home away from home."

On all sides of the valley, snow-covered peaks towered above them. Below, pine and fir trees bordered the flat, open field of snow. Frank could see a small cabin at the foot of one mountain. Smoke trailed from its chimney.

"Someone lives out here?" he asked.

"We do—sort of." Tom pulled off his pack and removed the snowboard he carried in it. "It's an old trapper's cabin. Justin and Bill and I found it and fixed it up. We keep food and wood out here. Bill uses it during hunting season, and if we're 'boarding until late, we crash."

"Very cool," Joe said. "So how do we get down?"

Tom smiled, showing the gap between his teeth. "There's only one way down, Joe. You should know that."

Frank followed Tom and Joe to a spot in the clearing where there was a wide run carved out of

71

the mountain. It was rougher than a ski run, and Frank could see a lot of boulders and trees in the way, but it was doable. If you knew what you were doing, that is. . . .

Tom strapped his feet into his board; Joe did the same. Frank didn't have official snowboarding boots, but Tom had told him he could use his regular hiking shoes.

"Just make sure they're strapped in tight," he told Frank. "You won't be able to feel the board so well, but go slow and you'll get the hang of it."

Frank nodded. Joe was already on his board and heading down the trail. From skateboarding, Frank knew the basic principles of snowboarding. He also knew, watching Tom go down, that the guy rode goofy—left foot forward.

"Figures," Frank said to himself. "Everything about the guy is a little funny."

While Joe and Tom carved wide turns on the run, and used the boulders to grab air, Frank stuck to the simple stuff. He figured out how to get momentum on the trail and how to control the board. He fell flat more than once and found himself face first in the icy snow, but eventually he got a rhythm going.

"Next time, try some moves," Tom urged him, once they were at the bottom of the trail.

"Sure," Frank said, feeling he was ready. "What should I start with?"

"How about a switch-stance mctwist with a back-end flip," Tom said.

"A what?" Frank asked.

"Never mind." Joe punched Tom on the arm. "Don't make him feel stupid," he said to Tom. "Everyone has to start somewhere."

Tom started the hike back up the trail. Joe followed him, and Frank took up the rear. Tom and Joe were already halfway up the mountain, when Frank saw a blur of brown in the woods on his right. He held back a moment to get a closer look.

It had to be an animal, Frank thought, especially once he saw that it was moving. He heard the sound of branches rustling and twigs breaking underfoot. From his experience camping, Frank knew that whatever was in there had to be big. Mice and squirrels didn't make much noise at all. But this thing sounded loud enough to be human.

Frank backed away, realizing he could be in serious trouble. But it was too late. The animal had seen him and was charging out of the woods.

Two seconds later Frank was face-to-face with a large brown bear.

8 Yet Another Suspect

Frank stood stock still.

Pretend you're a tree. Don't let him hear you breathe. Bears are really nearsighted. If you don't move, he won't know you're here.

All this was from Bear Survival 101, but Frank had no idea if what he'd read about how to live through a bear attack was true.

I'm about to find out.

The plan nearly worked. The bear lumbered forward a few steps, sniffed the air, and then, puzzled, stared in Frank's direction. Frank held his breath, but the bear didn't come any farther. Then Frank heard his brother and Tom up ahead, calling out his name.

"Frank!" Joe cried. "Look out. There's a bear down there!"

Duh, Joe, Frank thought, gritting his teeth. What would I do without you?

The bear looked to Frank as though it would be about six feet tall if it reared up. Its brown fur was thick; there were leaves and twigs stuck in it. From where he stood, Frank got a good whiff of bear odor, which was not unlike smelly feet. The bear yawned wide, and Frank got an up-close-and-personal view of the inside of his mouth.

That sure is one ugly mug, he thought.

And then, from the bottom of the trail, Frank heard two more voices. "Tom? Is that you? Where are you, man?"

"Up here," Tom cried. "Justin! Bill!"

Frank silently wished everyone would keep it down—the loud voices might rile the bear. Just then, as if it had read his mind, the bear reared up on its hind legs and let out a huge roar.

Oh, boy, Frank thought. Here goes.

Frank was just about to turn and make a run for it when Justin Greeley and Bill Forman came trudging up the trail.

"Uh-oh," Justin said, stopping short.

"That's a big one," Bill agreed.

"Keep it down," Frank whispered.

A second later Tom and Joe pulled up on their boards. The bear was lurching around in the snow now, obviously upset.

75

"Whoa," Tom said. He quickly unfastened his boots from his board and added, "Okay, here's what we do. Bill, you and Justin stand on that side of Frank. Do it, guys—now!"

Bill and Justin came over to Frank. Tom grabbed Joe and pulled him toward the group. The bear reared up again, and everybody froze.

"Now," Tom said, without taking his eyes from the bear, "wave your arms in the air. And shout— loud." Tom waved his hands above his head. "Like this. Yeoooaaahhh! Grrrrreaaahhh!"

Justin and Bill started shouting. Frank and Joe did the same. Together, the five guys pretended they were one huge monster, full of noise and movement. The bear dropped back down to all four legs. Then it edged backward in the snow. Taking one last look at the group, the bear lumbered back into the woods.

"It worked," Frank said, feeling his heartbeat slow down to a manageable rate. "He's gone."

"Of course he's gone," Tom said proudly. "That's how you scare off a bear."

"I thought you were supposed to stand still and play dead," Frank said.

"Wrong," Justin said. "Tom's got the right idea."

Bill yanked on his baseball cap and made a face. "I think Frank's right, to tell you the truth. That's what I always learned."

"Hey, guys," Joe said. "What does it matter?

76

We're safe, and the bear's gone. And I suggest we get out of here before he comes back."

"I'm with you," Frank said. He checked his watch. "Besides, it's almost eight-thirty. We should be heading into town."

"I'm gonna be late for work," Bill said.

"Me, too," Justin added.

The five boys hiked back up the trail and headed into the canyon. On the way back into Evergreen, Bill started talking about the robbery at the bank.

"I know Justin here saw Mitch leave the bank," Bill said. "But personally, I still think George could have set him up."

"George is a definite suspect," Frank said. "And so is Rob Rubel."

"Rubel?" Justin asked. "Because of that money he was spending in the shop yesterday?"

"Exactly," Joe said.

Justin shrugged a shoulder as he lumbered along on the trail. "I see what you're getting at, but the truth is I know what I saw. Mitch Taylor came out of the alley next to the trust company right after the alarm went off. And he was in a real hurry."

"We found a stash of money in Mitch's snowmobile," Tom put in. He stopped short on the trail to tell Bill and Justin. "Frank and Joe think someone may have framed Mitch."

"No kidding?" Justin looked at the Hardys in surprise. He pushed his orange-shaded sunglasses back up on his nose and rubbed the side of his face. "You're saying whoever robbed the bank planted that money in Mitch's snowmobile?"

"Could be," Frank said.

The group had reached the fork in the trail. To the right, the fire road led to First Street and the center of Evergreen. To the left, the road went on up to Mitch's cabin. Frank realized that to get around in Evergreen, he and Joe should return to Mitch's place and get his spare snowmobile.

"Catch you guys later," Joe said to Bill, Justin, and Tom. "Maybe we can get in some action after work?"

"Sounds cool," Justin agreed. "I think Len's taking a group of skiers out later this afternoon, around five. Maybe he can drop us off in Secret Valley on his way out. I'll ask."

"Great," Frank said.

"Be there," Bill said.

Back at Mitch's cabin, Frank and Joe jumped on the snowmobile. Ten minutes later they were passing Bill, Tom, and Justin on the road back into Evergreen. Frank realized that it was after nine o'clock and neither Justin nor Bill was even close to being at work. Either they were used to getting into trouble or they didn't care, or both.

At the sheriff's station, Mitch looked happy to see Frank and Joe. "That had to be the worst night of my life," he told the two brothers once they were alone in the tiny visitors' area. A guard was right outside the door, but otherwise Frank and Joe could talk to Mitch without being overheard.

The three of them sat down at a rickety table in the middle of the room. Frank didn't waste any time. "We know about the money, Mitch," he said.

Mitch seemed surprised. He looked up at Frank. "What money?"

"The money you hid in the snowmobile," Joe said.

Mitch glanced back and forth between Frank and Joe. "Uh. I was going to tell you guys——"

"When?" Frank asked. "What do you know about it?"

"I found it yesterday afternoon," Mitch said. "I was going to start salvaging the snowmobile. It was too wrecked to save. I unscrewed the back panel and found the dough." Mitch tugged his beard. "I was scared. I didn't know what to do. I realize it looks bad."

"It does," Frank agreed. "The sheriff came and impounded the snowmobile."

"What?" Mitch exclaimed. "How'd he find out about it?"

"We told him," Joe said. "We had to, Mitch."

Mitch dropped his head. "I guess you did," he said sullenly. "But that doesn't help my case."

There was silence in the room for several minutes. Finally, Frank said, "You know we want to

79

help you, Mitch, but we need to be sure that you're innocent. Holding back on us is no way to help your case."

"I know, I know." Mitch drew in a deep breath. "I'm sorry. It was stupid. But I'm telling you, I didn't rob that trust company. I left work at six. I overheard the sheriff tell someone yesterday that the alarm sounded right *after* six, so that lets me off the hook, doesn't it? It's three miles down that mountain and into town, and another two out to my cabin. I couldn't have gotten down here that fast."

"Maybe." Frank thought for a moment. "Can you prove you left work at six?"

"I lost my watch in the accident," Mitch said suddenly. "I didn't have it when we got back to the cabin, and now I'm sure it's got to be in the snow where I crashed. If the watch stopped when I crashed, then it could prove what time I got there, and that would prove I couldn't have been near the bank just after six, right?"

"I suppose," Joe said. "How long would it have taken you to get from town to the spot where you crashed?"

"That would be five miles all together. I'd say at least ten, fifteen minutes," Mitch said.

"And when did the sheriff say the alarm went off?" Frank asked.

"Six oh two," Mitch said.

"So *if* the accident made your watch stop, and *if* it stopped any time before six-ten, or so, then I guess we could argue that you couldn't have been at the bank just after six," Frank said.

"That's a lot of if's," Mitch said.

"It sure is," Frank said. "But we'll look for the watch anyway."

Mitch thought for a moment. "Didn't you say that sometimes amnesia victims get their memory back if they reenact the events leading up to the memory loss?" Mitch asked.

"I did read that," Frank said.

"Maybe we can get the sheriff to let Mitch reenact the events of that morning," Joe said, following Mitch's argument.

"Now that he's in custody, I doubt it," Frank said. "But I guess it's worth a try." He stood up. "We can ask him now."

"I wish I could remember more," Mitch said. "I told you about the red ski cap, though, didn't I?"

"No," Frank said slowly. This was getting frustrating. "What about the red ski cap?"

"I can't believe I didn't tell you!" Mitch exclaimed. "I'm a wreck. Anyway, I remember seeing a guy in a red ski cap leaning over me after the crash, before I passed out, I guess." Mitch paused, deep in thought. "But that's all I remember so far."

"You're sure?" Joe asked.

"Yes. Positive. Honestly." He laughed. "I know you don't believe me, but it's the truth. I did know about the money, and I saw a guy in a red ski cap right after the accident."

"Someone must have come along and found you before we did," Frank said, mulling over this latest turn of events.

"Do you think that person also planted the cash?" Joe asked.

"Could be." Frank signaled to the guard. "We'll be in touch. We're going to check out whatever we can about George DuPuy's financial situation and look into Rubel, too."

"DuPuy banks at the Evergreen Trust Company," Mitch said. "I know a woman who works there, Heather Harper. Tell her you're friends of mine. Maybe she can help."

"Thanks," Frank said.

Frank, Joe, and Mitch left the room. The guard escorted Mitch back to his cell, while Frank and Joe went in search of Sheriff Overton. The man was having coffee in his office. When he saw Frank and Joe, he beckoned them inside.

"There was five thousand dollars in that snowmobile," he informed them. "We're doing a trace now to see if it came from the Evergreen Trust Company. If it did, I'm going to get a search warrant and head out to Mitch's cabin. We'll find the other forty-five thousand that was taken, believe me."

"What if Mitch isn't your man?" Frank asked.

"He is," Overton told them. "He is."

"Just to be sure, how would you feel about letting Mitch out of jail to reenact the events of the morning the robbery took place?" Joe asked.

The sheriff sputtered on the sip of coffee he'd taken. "Are you kidding?" he asked. "What for?"

Frank explained their theory about how it might jar Mitch's memory.

"No way," Overton stated flatly. "Mitch Taylor's prints matched the ones we found on the back door of the savings and loan building. They weren't on the safe, but even so, he's staying right where he is until I get enough evidence for an indictment, and then he's going to trial."

Seeing that they weren't going to make any headway with Sheriff Overton, Frank and Joe said goodbye and headed over to the bank. At the entrance to the condos that shared the same building as the Evergreen Trust Company, Frank spotted a couple in ski clothes. Otherwise, the streets were fairly empty. Maybe Evergreen got crowded during the height of the ski season, but right now it seemed like a pretty sleepy town.

At the bank, Frank and Joe found Heather Harper, a loan officer, at her desk. The young woman was surprised to hear that Frank and Joe were helping Mitch prove his innocence in the robbery, but glad, too.

"I know he didn't do it," she said, giving the Hardys an intense stare with her clear blue eyes. "Whatever I can do to help Mitch, I will. We go way back."

"Actually, there is one thing you can do to help

us." Joe told her they were looking for information about George DuPuy's financial situation.

Heather looked over her shoulder and leaned in close to Frank and Joe. "That's confidential information. I could lose my job."

"Can you give us just yes or no answers to some questions we have?" Frank asked.

"I guess." Heather bit on her lower lip. "But you didn't hear anything from me."

"Is George in financial trouble?" Joe asked.

"From what I've heard, yes," Heather said.

"And it has to do with his business?" Frank put in.

"Yes, it does," Heather told them.

"You're a loan officer," Joe said. "Is the bank going to foreclose on George?"

Heather drew in a sharp breath. "We were. Until George promised us he'd make a substantial payment on an outstanding short-term loan he has with us, and we gave him a temporary extension. That wasn't yes or no, but that's what you want to hear, right?"

"Yes, it is," Joe said. "How substantial?"

"A lot," Heather said.

"More than forty thousand?" Frank asked.

"Yes."

"But less than fifty?" Joe asked.

"How did you know?" Heather asked. Frank turned to his brother, following the line of reasoning. If George stole the money from the bank and stashed five thousand in Mitch's snowmobile, he'd have less than fifty thousand left over to pay back his loan. Was this the "ship coming in" that Bill Forman had heard George talking about?

"Thank you," Frank said to Heather.

Heather stood up and shook both their hands. "It's for Mitch, and I owe him. But as I told you, if anyone wants to know who gave you this information, it wasn't me."

As the Hardys left the bank, Frank tried to make sense of this latest lead. "There's something that's bothering me. If DuPuy did rob the bank, then did he also plan to frame Mitch, or was that just a lucky break?"

Joe shook his head. "How could DuPuy have known Mitch would ride by at the exact moment the bank was being robbed? And another thing—if Mitch was framed, the person who did it couldn't have counted on Mitch losing his memory."

"True enough." Frank and Joe stood outside the bank. The sun was shining, and it was a pretty day, if a little cold. A half-dozen cars were parked on Main Street, and some tourists strolled the sidewalk in front of the café. From the street, where the snowmobile was parked, Frank heard the sound of a voice coming through on the two-way radio. "It's got to be Con," he said to Joe. "Come on."

Frank had the radio stashed in his pack, which

he'd slung over the back of the seat. He went to retrieve it and recognized Con Riley's voice coming through.

"Frank, Con Riley here," the man said. "Are you there? Come in, Frank, this is Con."

"Con, we're here," Frank said. "You got something for us?"

"I sure do," Con announced. "That guy Rubel, he sure does have a record."

"For what?" Frank Hardy asked.

"You're not going to believe this," Con told him. "Bank robbery."

9 Hot on the Trail

"So now Rubel's our main suspect?" Joe asked his brother, once Frank had finished speaking with Con. "Or do we stick with DuPuy?"

"Don't forget that Mitch still isn't in the clear," Frank said. "A lot of his story isn't stacking up very logically, if you ask me."

"Yeah. That memory loss is proving to be very convenient for Mitch," Joe observed.

"Exactly," Frank said.

While the Hardys were standing outside the trust company, Joe noticed an armored car parked in the alley next to the building. Now the car pulled out onto the street, but a steel door in the side of the bank remained slightly ajar.

"We never did get a chance to look at that vault,

did we?" he asked Frank, keeping his eyes on the door.

"No. Why?" Frank wanted to know.

"Maybe we have our shot now." With that, Joe headed down the alley and pulled open the door, which was still slightly ajar. When he stepped inside, he saw why the driver of the armored car didn't mind leaving the door open.

Joe was standing in a vestibule, staring at another door that led to the vault itself. And that door was locked shut.

"You didn't really think we'd be able to just step inside the vault area, did you?" Frank asked his brother.

Joe scowled. "No. But maybe we can learn a few things anyway."

Joe checked out the lock on the door that led to the vault. Alarm wires ran from the wall of the bank to the vault. They were still cut and dangling from the break-in. To Joe's trained eye, the lock definitely looked as if someone—probably the bank robber—had broken in this way. There were scratch marks on the cylinder.

"Looks as if the bank hasn't made any repairs since the robbery," Frank said.

"They probably don't want to erase the evidence yet," Joe guessed. Next, Joe checked out the surroundings. The vestibule was a small brick room, the size of a closet. Before him was the door that led to the vault. Behind him was the door he'd come through. To his right was another door, and the alarm wires connected to this door had been severed also. Joe checked the doorknob. "Locked," he said to Frank.

"Maybe not for long," Frank said. He drew out his lock-pick tool and set to work. Within a few minutes he had the door open, and he and Joe descended some stairs into a basement.

"It seems like a real breach in security to have this basement here, wouldn't you say?" Joe observed. "Anyone could cut their way through the ceiling into the vault."

"Maybe," Frank said. "But my guess is the whole bank floor is probably alarmed."

The basement ran the length of the building. It was dimly lit with bare, overhead bulbs. There were pieces of scrap wood stacked around, and other construction debris. Joe remembered the sign for the condos that were renting in the floors above the bank.

"They must have just finished renovating this place," Joe said. "The trust company probably figured it could make money by converting the rest of the building into ski condos." Joe followed the bank's main electrical wiring through a maze of rooms and hallways.

"I wonder why the wires to both doors were cut," Frank said as he followed Joe.

"Maybe the robber didn't know which door was the one to the vault?" Joe suggested.

Frank was silent for a moment, and Joe knew some idea was hatching in his brain. Finally Frank said, "Wouldn't the alarm go off as soon as the wires were cut?"

"Sure," Joe said.

"And wouldn't the police arrive at that point?"

"I guess so," Joe admitted.

"So how did the thief have time to rob the bank while the alarm was going off?" Frank asked.

"I don't know," Joe said in exasperation. "Isn't that what we're down here trying to figure out?" In the dim basement, Joe reasoned out the puzzle. "Justin says Mitch rode by just after the alarm sounded. Was there enough time for Mitch to trip the alarm and then rob the bank and get away? We'll have to ask Justin what he thinks."

Following the wiring, Joe reached the end of a long passageway. There, a set of stairs went up. Joe and Frank climbed them and found they'd reached the ground floor of the condos that shared the building with the Evergreen Trust Company. Just before he pushed open the door all the way, Joe saw an old circuit breaker on the wall of the stairwell, and a newer one next to it that hadn't yet been hooked up. On the old circuit breaker, there were two switches. A label next to one switch read, Warehouse, and another read Bank.

Joe let out a low whistle. "I think I know how our robber cut those wires without tripping the alarm," he said to Frank. "He flipped the power off for the whole building. That gave him the chance to get into the bank, cut the wires, and get inside."

"Clever," Frank said. He pointed to the newer fuse box. "My guess is that the bank knew it would have a problem sharing electricity with the condos. It was probably getting ready to take the electricity off the same line—"

"But the robber struck first," Joe said. "Just in time."

"So if we find out who lives here," Frank said, "and who knew about this circuit breaker—"

"We'll have a good lead on a solid suspect," Joe finished. "What do you bet it's Rob Rubel?"

Joe entered the ground floor hallway and quickly found the apartment building's mailboxes by the front door.

"Bingo!" he said to Frank, pointing out Rubel's name on a mailbox. "There's our man."

"I'm surprised Sheriff Overton hasn't figured this one out," Frank said.

"Obviously, he hasn't," Joe said. "Or else he'd be onto Rubel, too." He ran his eyes over the other names on the mailboxes. "Hey, check it out. Bill lives here, also."

Frank recognized Bill's name on a mailbox. "We should ask him about that morning, and if the power went off around six."

"Right." Joe made a note of Rubel's apartment number. "Meanwhile, let's pay Rob a friendly visit."

"It would be even friendlier if he wasn't home," Frank said.

"I think I see what you're driving at," Joe said, a smile spreading across his face.

There were six condos in the building. Rob's was number four, and Frank and Joe found it on the second floor. Joe knocked loudly. When there was no answer, Frank took out his lock-pick kit and went to work.

"Presto," Frank said, leading the way inside Rob's apartment. The place was a mess. Piles of clothes lay everywhere, along with stacks of dirty dishes. Amid all the trash, Joe noticed several brand-new items: a mountain bike; a stereo, still in its box; and a new television.

"He sure isn't hiding the wealth, is he?" Joe asked.

"Not exactly. Check this out." Frank had pulled a desk drawer open. Joe stepped over a half-empty pizza box to see a stack of hundred-dollar bills in the drawer.

"Yowza," he said. "Could he be any more obvious, do you think?"

Frank removed one of the bills and put it in his wallet.

"What gives?" Joe asked. "Got your eye on a new pair of skis, too?"

"Very funny. I want to have Heather Harper run a trace on this money. She should be able to tell us if it was part of the cash that was stolen from the bank."

"Got it." Joe looked around the apartment and let out a long sigh. "I think it's time to have a long chat with Rob Rubel."

"I couldn't agree with you more," Frank said.

The Hardys hunted around Rob's apartment for more clues, but fifteen minutes later they were ready to give up. The only other worthwhile detail they noticed was that Rob's skis were missing, which meant he was probably on the slopes. They pulled the door shut behind them and headed out the front entrance to the condos. Frank stopped in the bank next door and dropped the hundred dollar bill off with Heather Harper. Then he and Joe stopped for lunch. They realized they hadn't eaten since early that morning. It was one o'clock in the afternoon, and they were starving. After a quick burger at the café, Frank and Joe rented ski gear from Justin and headed back up Mount Summit in search of Rob Rubel.

At the top of Headwall, one of the expert runs, Joe recognized a few of Rob's friends from the day before. He skied over to the short one with the curly dark hair whose name was Dan.

"Do us a favor," Joe said. "You're friends with Rob Rubel, right?"

Dan nodded noncommittally. "So?" he asked.

"Tell him Frank and Joe Hardy are looking for him," he said. "He can find us on the slope."

"If I see him," Dan said sullenly. "But I'm not in charge of the guy."

For the next half hour, Joe and Frank kept their eyes peeled for Rob. They skied the run several times, and rode the lifts looking for him, but they didn't see Rob anywhere on Headwall.

"The guy's nowhere around," Frank said in frustration. "We should just head back to the ski rental shop and wait for Bill and Justin."

Joe agreed. "We're wasting our time up here. Except for the skiing, that is."

Frank took the lead down the slope. Joe was fast behind him, though, and together the Hardys negotiated the steep top section of Headwall. They were cruising the lower part of the run, when they heard a voice calling their names.

"Hey, Frank! Joe! I heard you were looking for me!"

Joe turned on his skis to see Rob Rubel coming up fast. With him were a half-dozen of his ski bum buddies. The group was headed right for the brothers, and they were forcing every other skier in their path out of the way.

"Uh-oh," Frank said. "Looks like trouble."

"Let's get out of here," Joe said. "Rob's not in a mood to answer questions. He's in a mood to bust some heads."

Frank pushed off; Joe was close behind. It was a tense moment. The slope was more crowded than it had been the day before. Frank and Joe didn't have

94

much room to maneuver. Rob, Dan, and the others were hot on their trail.

"He's trying to run us off the slope," Joe said, pushing himself harder as he tried to grab a fast edge on his skis.

"Well, don't let him," Frank said.

Joe looked to his left. Rob and the others were skiing alongside him now, and the group was forming a tight knot. Dan led the pack, cutting Frank closer toward the edge of the slope.

Rob grabbed the rear of the group. He skied fast behind Joe, tormenting him at each turn.

"Give it up, Joey boy," Rob said with a nasty grin. "You can't handle the pressure."

By now Dan had forced Frank way off course. Joe couldn't hold his own against Rob, either.

The next thing Joe knew, he was losing control in the rough, ungroomed snow that bordered the run. He tried hard to keep control, but he knew it was a losing battle.

Suddenly Joe felt himself lose his edge. He tried to get a grip on the slick snow, but it was useless. He'd lost control and was heading off the slope—straight for the woods.

10 A 'Boarder's Paradise

Out of the corner of his eye, Frank saw his brother go flying off the trail. Then he heard Joe cry out. But there was nothing Frank could do to help Joe now. Rob was skiing hard right beside him.

"You're next, Frank. Ready, set—go!"

With that, Rob and Dan and all the others closed in on Frank. "So you think you're a hot shot, huh?" Dan cried out. "Let's see you prove it, Frank."

Dan swerved into him. Frank kept his weight low and swiftly edged out of the way. Rob skied out from the back of the group and tried a similar maneuver. Once again, Frank was able to stay on course.

By now the group was headed into the lower section of the run. There were a lot more skiers here—and a lot more witnesses, too. Rob must have seen that it was a bad idea to keep harassing Frank, because he backed off.

"Chill out, guys," Rob said, pulling away from the group.

Dan scowled and kept the pressure on, skiing close to Frank. "I'm not done with him."

"I am," Rubel insisted loudly. "Leave him alone. There are too many people down here, Dan. You want to get blackballed?"

"You're a wimp, Rubel," Dan said, pulling back. "Remind me not to hang out with you again."

With that, Dan peeled away and skied off. Rubel made a face, then tucked into a crouch. "See ya, Frank," Rubel said.

"Not so fast, bud," Frank muttered through gritted teeth. He crouched down over his skis and followed Rob through the maze of other skiers. He finally caught up with the guy by the lodge at the base of the mountain. Rob was busy taking off his skis and unfastening his boots.

"Now that you've had your fun," Frank told Rob, "let me lay it out for you. One, you're a prime suspect in the robbery at the Evergreen Trust Company. Two, I want to know where you were the morning of the robbery. And three, how did you happen to come by all the money you've been spending?"

Rob stood his skis beside him and looked at Frank for a long moment. Then a smile appeared on his deeply tanned face. "Well, well, well," he said. "Just to prove what idiots you guys really are, I'll give you a few answers, Frank. One, everyone knows the money came from my grandfather, who died recently. And two, I've got a copy of his will back at my place, if you want to see it."

Frank held his ground. "I might. Meanwhile, can you prove you weren't in town that morning?"

"Sure I can." Rob smiled as he reached for his wallet. He drew out a ticket stub. "I was in Calgary the night before, and I got on a bus early that morning. Check out the date."

Frank did and saw that the ticket was for the day the bank was robbed. "I'll have to look into the bus schedule," he said, handing the ticket stub back to Rob.

"Go ahead, but you'll feel pretty stupid when you do," Rob said, smiling even wider. "What I'm telling you is the truth, Frank. Sorry." He reached over to pat Frank condescendingly on the arm. "Guess you're back to square one. But at least now you know you've got the wrong guy. And you also know that next time you and your brother try to come after me, you'll both end up kissing that mountain face first, and you'll never ski again."

"Nice guy," Frank muttered as Rob walked away. He and Joe really were back to square one. . . .

Joe!

His brother lay up on the trail somewhere. He could be hurt. Frank set off toward the ski patrol headquarters, which he remembered seeing near one of the main lifts. He was just about to ask for help when he spotted Joe coming down the mountain, strapped to the back of a red ski patrol snowmobile.

"Thanks for ditching me," Joe said with a grin.

"Sorry. I had problems of my own," Frank said.

The ski patrol guide handed Joe's skis and poles to Frank. "It looks like he twisted his ankle. I don't think it's bad, but I thought I'd bring him down the mountain anyway."

"Thanks," Frank said. He helped Joe from the back of the snowmobile. "Can you walk?"

Joe stepped on his bad ankle. "No problem. I twisted it when I fell, but it hardly hurts at all."

"You were lucky," Frank said.

"Tell me about it." Joe made a face. "I don't know who's the biggest creep, Rubel or his friends."

While they headed back to Mitch's spare snowmobile, Frank told his brother what he'd learned from Rob Rubel.

"Do you believe him?" Joe asked.

Frank shrugged. "We can check it out."

Joe kicked a piece of ice across the parking lot and said, "He was a prime suspect."

"There's still DuPuy," Frank reminded his brother.

"What are we going to do about George?" Joe asked.

Frank thought for a moment. "We need to know more about that loan he's going to pay back. Where did the money come from?"

"We know where he keeps his books," Joe reminded Frank. "We saw him put them in the safe. We can break into the trailer, crack the safe, and see what we can learn from the books."

"There's only one problem with that plan," Frank said.

"What's that?" Joe asked.

"Why would DuPuy write it down in his books if the money came from a bank robbery?" Frank asked.

"He'd have to account for the money somehow," Joe said. "And he'd have to indicate how he came by the cash to pay back the loan. Even if it's a lie."

"True," Frank said. He started up the snowmobile once Joe was safely on board. "I guess it's worth a shot."

"Of course it is," Joe said.

On the way back to Mount Summit Ski Rentals, Frank also reminded Joe that they had to find out if Rob's story about inheriting the money from his grandfather was true or not.

"We can ask Tom what he's heard," Joe told him.

It was only three, and the Hardys were a bit early to meet Justin and Bill, so they dropped off the skis and grabbed a snack at the café. By three-thirty they were standing outside the rental shop, ready to head out in the helicopter. Justin came out to greet them, and Bill and Tom appeared a few minutes later.

"Ready for the ride of your lives?" Justin asked Frank and Joe.

"You bet we are," Frank told him.

The group went around to the back of the shop, where Len Grossman was just climbing into the cockpit of the helicopter. Justin introduced Frank and Joe to the burly older man.

"So I'm giving you kids a ride out to Secret Valley, huh?" Grossman asked. "Hop on board."

Within minutes, Len was piloting them up into the air above the lot behind the ski rental shop. The copter sat five comfortably, and Frank's window seat gave him a terrific view of the mountains as they flew.

"It'll get dark soon," Len told them. "You kids better not stay out too long."

Tom still had his spare snowboard for Frank, and Joe had borrowed one from Justin at the shop. Justin and Bill both had motorized contraptions for their boards like the one Tom's father had built for him.

"So when's your dad going to make one for us?" Frank asked.

Tom smiled. "He's working on 'em. I got him started already."

"Not to change the subject or anything, but what's going on with Mitch and the robbery?" Bill asked from his seat next to Len. "Any more leads?"

101

"We sneaked into Rob's place today—" Frank started to say.

"You did?" Justin asked eagerly. He was sitting beside Joe in the seat in front of Frank. "What did you learn?"

Frank remembered to ask Bill about the possible power outage the morning of the robbery. Bill thought for a moment, then said, slowly, "You know, I think it's possible. That morning, my alarm didn't go off, and when I finally did wake up, I saw that the alarm clock was blinking at twelve o'clock. You know how it does that if the power goes out?"

Frank felt his excitement rising. "We think that's how the robber got into the bank without setting off the alarm."

"But I heard the alarm go off," Justin said. "Then I saw Mitch cruising down Main Street."

"Maybe someone came along and tripped the switch," Joe put in. "And the alarm went off then."

"It's something to think about," Frank said. "Anyway, we found a stash of money in Rob's drawer, and we're running a trace on it. I confronted Rubel this afternoon. He said he'd inherited all his cash from his grandfather, who passed away recently."

"You guys know anything about that?" Joe asked.

Tom ran a hand through his red hair. "No," he said, "but maybe my dad can help you find out. When he's not making motors for my snowboard, he's a lawyer in Banff."

"Cool," Frank said, nodding. "That's exactly the help we need. See if your dad can find out if Rob came into an inheritance recently."

"No problem," Tom said.

"What about DuPuy?" Bill asked.

Frank explained that he and Joe were going to check out DuPuy that night. "We've got a plan."

"Which we can discuss later, right?" Bill tilted his head toward Len.

"Right," Joe agreed.

"Here we go!" Len announced. "First stop, Secret Valley."

The man was coasting the copter onto a landing spot a third of the way down into Secret Valley. The view of the valley below was incredible. As the copter landed, first Justin, then Tom, then Bill, and finally Frank and Joe hopped out. With a thumbs-up sign from Justin, Len lifted back up, leaving the group alone.

"Wow," Frank said.

"Double wow," Joe agreed.

No lift had ever gotten Frank up so high, or into such pure snow. It was still only November, but the snow coverage out in the valley was terrific. Below them, it was a clear, beautiful run down the mountain. Tom, Justin, and Bill were already shoving off. Joe strapped himself into his board and, with a yell, went down.

Frank waited a second longer, until the group

had disappeared from sight. Then he too dug into the long, white run.

It was amazing. Even with Tom, Justin, Bill, and Joe, Frank still had half a mountainside to himself. There wasn't anyone else around for miles, and Frank took his time getting down the mountain.

At the bottom, Joe, Bill, Tom, and Justin were waiting. Tom's face was even redder than usual, and all four boys were flushed with excitement.

"Incredible," Joe said, looking back up the mountain at their tracks. "What a ride."

"You're not kidding," Frank agreed.

"I bet you wish you could 'board like this all the time," Tom said.

"Nah," Frank said with a smile. "I wouldn't want to get spoiled."

The group headed toward the trail that led out of the valley. Now that the sun was setting, the air had turned cold, and all five agreed it was time to hike out.

Joe and Tom were in the lead. Justin hiked in the middle, and Bill took up the rear, along with Frank.

"What I wanted to tell you back there in the copter is that I think I know where George keeps the spare key to the safe," Bill said. "It's taped to the underside of his top desk drawer. And I know for a fact that he keeps his books in the safe."

"Great!" Frank said. Bill was handing them a lucky break. "Joe and I wanted to check out George's books, as a matter of fact."

"I know Justin thinks Mitch is the guilty one," Bill said, "but personally, my bets are on George. I hope this gives you a lead you can use."

"It sure does," Frank said. "Joe and I are going to head up there tonight. Thanks!"

Frank caught up to Joe at the front of the group and told him about the lead Bill had given them.

"That's great," Joe agreed. "You know, while we were hiking, I remembered that we promised Mitch we'd look for his watch."

"How's that going to help you?" Justin asked.

"Mitch is hoping that the accident made his watch stop. Depending on the time it stopped, we'll know if he could have been at the bank at six oh two, when the alarm went off," Joe explained.

"Unless he left work early," Justin observed.

Frank trudged along on the trail, winded from the climb. For a while, no one spoke. They hiked up into the canyon and along the path to the spot where it intersected the fire road. Tom wanted to head home, so he said a quick goodbye to Frank and Joe and joined Justin and Bill on the fire road back to Evergreen. Frank and Joe took the road on up to Mitch's cabin, stopping first at the spot where Mitch had had his accident.

Frank quickly found the tree Mitch had crashed into. He and Joe spent a few minutes digging in the snow around the site.

"If you were a watch, where would you spend your free time?" Joe asked.

Frank groaned at his brother's bad joke, and doubled back on the road a few steps. "It's getting dark," he said. "We're not going to find anything out here. Come on, we'll look again in the morning."

"Not necessarily." Joe stood up from the spot where he'd been kneeling. Frank shone his penlight on Joe. In his brother's hand was a man's watch. "And guess what?" Joe asked, checking the time. "It's not late at all. According to this watch, it's still only six oh five."

"If the alarm went off at six oh two, Mitch couldn't have been at the bank then," Frank reasoned. "He'd never make it out here in only three minutes."

"Is this enough proof to convince Sheriff Overton to let Mitch reenact the crime?" Joe wondered aloud.

"Maybe," Frank said.

Suddenly Joe took a few steps off the trail and into the woods.

"Where are you going?" Frank asked.

"If this doesn't convince him, nothing will." Joe emerged from the woods and held out a red ski hat. "It was buried in the snow, but not very well. My guess is the guy lost it, then took off without it."

Frank remembered what Mitch had said about a guy in a red ski hat hovering over him just after the accident. "Someone was here," he said. "Someone ran into Mitch, maybe after his accident. Maybe that someone helped cause the accident."

Joe pocketed Mitch's watch and the ski cap. "Let's head back to the cabin and call Overton."

Back at Mitch's cabin, Joe put in the call to the sheriff while Frank packed a bag with gear. When Joe got off the phone a few minutes later, he had a broad smile on his face.

"Overton agrees the facts don't line up," Joe said. "He's willing to let us take Mitch out, first thing tomorrow morning."

"All right!" Frank exclaimed. Somehow, he felt as if they were on their way to a break in the case. "Let's hope we turn up something at DuPuy's tonight. We could be close to cracking this thing."

Four hours later Frank and Joe had eaten dinner and were climbing over the gate at DuPuy Lumber Company. To avoid attracting attention, they'd parked the snowmobile in the woods just down the hill from the gate. Now, they hopped down off the gate and quickly made their way into DuPuy's trailer. Once inside, Frank found the key to the safe in exactly the spot where Bill had told them to look.

"You can do the honors," Frank said to Joe, handing him the key.

Joe put the key into the lock of the safe, turned the handle, and opened the safe door. Frank shone his penlight inside, giving both Hardys a firsthand view of stacks and stacks of hundred-, fifty-, and twenty-dollar bills. Each stack was neatly wrapped, as if it had come directly from a bank.

"Are you thinking what I'm thinking?" Frank asked Joe.

"That there's probably forty-five thousand dollars here," Joe said, "and that it came from the Evergreen Trust Company?"

"You bet."

Frank stepped closer. There was no way he and Joe could take the time to count the money to know exactly how much was there, but they could still check out George's accounting books, which were stacked on top of the money.

"Here you go," Frank said, handing one of the books to Joe. "Let's see what we can find out."

Frank was just about to sit down at DuPuy's desk when he heard footsteps out in the lumber yard.

"Joe!" Frank warned. "Get down!"

Suddenly there was a flash of light and a loud popping sound. The window right next to Frank exploded, and the glass shattered all over the desk.

"What's going on?" Joe asked, ducking quickly.

"There's someone out in the lumberyard," Frank said. "Someone shooting at us!"

11 Killer Logging
Truck II

Joe Hardy crept over to the shattered window. Being careful to stay low, he popped his head just over the frame. The lumberyard was dark, but as more shots rang out, flashes of light filled the air.

"I think our sniper is over by the gate," Joe said.

"There goes our escape route," Frank groaned.

One by one, the sniper was taking out each window of the trailer. With each pane of shattered glass, Frank flinched.

"Not a good situation," Joe agreed, leaning back against the wall. "There's no back door."

Frank played his penlight around the inside of DuPuy's trailer. "True," he said. "But there is a back window." He held the light on a window high

109

in the wall next to the desk. "Think we can make it?"

"It's our only shot," Joe said.

Frank groaned.

"Sorry," Joe said. "This is no time for a joke."

While Frank set George's desk chair by the window, Joe called out into the lumberyard. "We're coming out. Hold your fire. We don't want any trouble."

"Nice cover," Frank whispered. "Let's hope it works."

Frank and Joe climbed through the window in the back of the trailer. For several long minutes, the lumberyard was quiet. Now they were faced with the problem of how to sneak around behind the shooter to reach the gate. The fence was bordered with barbed wire, so there was no climbing over it. Joe inched around the edge of DuPuy's property, close to the fence, with Frank on his heels. The Hardys didn't use their flashlights, and they were careful to be as quiet as possible. For the most part, the heavy machinery parked in the yard gave them cover. But when they got close to the gate, Joe saw they had to make a run across the front of the yard without any protection.

"What'll we do?" he asked his brother.

Even with the dark as cover, they had a good hundred yards to run.

"Where's the sniper?" Frank asked. "I can't see him."

110

Joe made out a tall figure crossing the lumberyard from the gate to the trailer.

"He's going in," Joe said. "He must wonder why we haven't come out yet. Let's go!"

"Not so fast." Frank pulled on Joe's jacket. "Let's see what he does."

The guy headed for the trailer, spent less than two minutes inside, then came back out. He had a flashlight with him, and he beamed it into the yard. Frank and Joe kept low against the fence, but they didn't have quite enough cover. The beam of the flashlight caught the tops of their heads.

"Let's get out of here," Joe yelled. "Fast!"

Joe raced for the gate, vaulting over it in one leap. He didn't stop until they were at the snowmobile and Frank was firing it up. He turned once to see the guy running for one of the trucks parked in front of the mill.

"Hurry," Joe cried. "He's getting into one of the trucks."

Sure enough, a logging truck was pulling out of the lumberyard. The driver had to stop to open the gate, which gave the Hardys some extra time, but through the woods Joe could see the headlights of the logging truck beaming down upon them. Frank was hampered by the trees and the undergrowth in the forest and was frantically zigzagging around obstacles.

"Get us out of here," Joe said through clenched teeth.

"I'm trying," Frank said, ducking as a branch slapped him in the forehead.

Finally, he got the snowmobile out of the woods and onto the road. By this point, the logging truck was at the top of the grade above them and bearing down hard.

"How fast can this thing go?" Joe asked.

"Fifty," Frank said. "Sixty at the most."

"That's not good enough," Joe said.

"Don't you think I know that?" Frank gunned the engine, causing it to whine even louder. "Snowmobiles aren't made to outrun eighteen-wheelers."

"They should be," Joe said. "'Cause we're about to try."

"When I get to Evergreen, I'll take the fire road," Frank told his brother. "Maybe we can lose him on it."

"I hope so," Joe said.

Joe turned around to see that the truck was coming down the hill at what looked like a million miles an hour. He also saw a glint of steel in the darkness. When he heard a shot blaze past his ear, he knew they were in trouble.

"He's shooting at us again," Joe told his brother.

"I noticed."

Frank pushed the snowmobile even harder. They were going so fast, Joe didn't know if he could hold on. But it wasn't fast enough. The truck was right on their tail now, and there was no shaking it. Joe kept trying to look in the cab to see if it was DuPuy driving, but every time he did, the driver took another shot.

"Watch out," Joe warned.

They were coming up on a turnout, where the road widened to create a passing lane. "I'm going to have to go off-road," Frank yelled to Joe. "That's the only way we'll lose him."

"Do it," Joe said.

But just as Frank was about to head into the turnout, the driver used the extra room on the road to pull alongside them on the left. Joe had a more than closeup view of the logging truck and its heavy load of uncut logs.

"He's right there!" Joe cried. "Look out!"

Frank yanked the snowmobile hard to the right. At the same time, the driver of the truck lurched left. The swerve sent the truck's load of timber off balance.

Joe watched in horror as the ropes holding down the load snapped free. Suddenly all the timber was flying every which way off the truck. Log after log came catapulting through the air.

Joe held up his arms to protect himself. Unless Frank did something—fast—they were going to be buried alive.

12 The Reenactment

"Hold on tight!" Frank Hardy cried.

At the last second he got a final burst of power from the snowmobile—enough to propel them out of the path of the incoming logs.

"Keep down," Frank urged, planting himself low on the snowmobile's handlebars.

Frank pulled as hard as he could to the right. A falling log practically took them out from behind, but Frank managed to scoot free, just before it could pin them down. A second later Frank stared down some dark woods, hoping that somehow he'd find a path through them.

"Rough road ahead," he warned.

"Tell me about it," Joe gasped from behind.

The snowmobile pounded through the woods,

taking every spare branch with it. Holding out his right arm to protect his eyes from flying branches, Frank ducked and steered. Somehow he found enough room between the trees to get them safely off the road and away from the monster trucker.

"What was that guy's problem?" Joe demanded, once they had slowed down. "And where are we?"

"The foothills of beautiful Squaw Peak," Frank said, breathing hard. "Safe and sound."

"And lost. Do you think he's going to come chasing after us?" Joe asked, looking into the woods behind him.

"I doubt it. That guy—whoever he was—achieved his goal."

"Of what?" Joe asked.

"Scaring us off," Frank said. "Still, I think we'd better wait a little while before we head back out to the road. I want to be sure he's gone."

"You won't hear me arguing." Joe pulled his collar up around his ears. It wasn't too cold, just uncomfortable. "Too bad we didn't bring along some hot chocolate."

"We didn't know we'd be sitting in the middle of the woods in the middle of the night, did we?" Frank asked.

"No. But if we'd thought about it, we could have predicted something like this would happen. Next time, we're heading south for a vacation."

They waited a good hour before Frank steered them back through the woods and onto the road.

There was no sign of the mystery trucker, although the road was still full of fallen logs.

"I guess George will get one of his loggers out here to haul them back up to the lumberyard," Frank pointed out.

"So was that George just now?" Joe wondered aloud. "Or someone else who's got it in for us."

"Who knew we were going to be up here?" Frank said. "Bill, Justin, and Tom. If that was George in the truck, one of them would have had to tip him off."

"Maybe George came upon us by accident," Joe pointed out.

Frank revved the snowmobile and put it into gear. "Maybe. Let's hope our reenactment tomorrow morning gives us more clues. If not, we'll confront George openly with our suspicions and go from there. Right now, I'm too tired to think straight. Let's head back to Mitch's and call it a night."

Joe was up with a start at five the next morning. He and Frank had fallen into bed, exhausted, after midnight the night before.

"Less than five hours just isn't enough sleep," Joe mumbled to his brother as Frank walked through the cabin's darkened living room. "Why'd we have to schedule this thing so early?"

"Mitch gets off work at six," Frank reminded him. "We have to do this thing by the book."

"I know, I know." Joe stumbled to the bathroom. "I just hope this harebrained scheme works," he said.

Frank and Joe ate a quick breakfast of juice and cereal, and then headed out on Mitch's snowmobile. Sheriff Overton was going to lend them another snowmobile to use during the reenactment. By five-thirty, the Hardys were pulling up in front of the sheriff's station. Overton was already there, waiting to let them into the holding area outside Mitch's cell.

Mitch Taylor was still rubbing the sleep out of his weary eyes. "Mornin'," he said, stretching. "You boys ready?"

"You bet we are," Frank said. "Not to put too much pressure on you, Mitch, but we're counting on this reenactment to jar some facts loose in that brain of yours."

"Well, just the thought of it freed up something," Mitch told them.

"It did? You remembered what happened?" Joe asked with excitement.

"Not exactly." Mitch gave them a small embarrassed smile. "I remembered that I left work early that day. At five forty-five, to be precise—not six, as I told you."

Joe felt his stomach sink. "Fifteen whole minutes early!"

"You had enough time to leave work, rob the bank, and crash by six oh five," Frank said.

"But it doesn't explain why Justin said you left the bank just after six, when the alarm went off," Joe pointed out. "You still wouldn't have had enough time to rob the bank."

The sheriff confirmed Joe's thinking. "Our report—from Justin and the trust company's records—says the alarm went off at six oh two."

"Could Mitch get from the bank to the crash site in three minutes?" Joe asked.

Mitch thought for a moment. "Doubtful," he said. "But I guess we'll find out, won't we?" With that, he tied a scarf around his neck, and Overton let him out of his jail cell.

"We'll have him back by six-thirty," Frank said to the sheriff.

"I'm going to follow you kids," Overton said. "You think I'd let you take my prime suspect out of my eyesight for even five minutes?"

"I guess not," Joe said.

The group headed out of the sheriff's station and onto the street. Mitch and Joe got onto the lead snowmobile, with Joe driving, while Frank and the sheriff rode behind. They drove down Main Street and up into the mountains. By just before five-forty, they were at the entrance to the Land and Forest Services, where Mitch worked. At five forty-five on the dot, Mitch directed Joe back down the mountain and onto Main Street.

Along the way, Joe realized that it made sense that Justin was the only witness. At this hour, the town was completely asleep. The sun was just rising on the mountains to his right. Even the café didn't open until six-thirty.

"You picking up on anything?" Joe turned to ask Mitch.

"Nothing yet," Mitch said. "Keep going."

Joe checked his watch. "Five fifty-two," he told Mitch.

A minute later they were passing the sheriff's station on their left. The ski resort was on their right. Then they came to the Evergreen Trust Company.

"Slow down," Mitch said. Joe slowed to a crawl. Mitch was gazing intently into the bank's storefront window. "Stop," Mitch commanded.

Joe stopped the snowmobile. Slowly Mitch got off the back and began walking toward the bank.

"What's going on?" Frank asked, pulling to a stop beside Joe.

"I think something's coming back to him," Joe whispered.

By now Mitch was standing right in front of the trust company. "I just remembered; I saw something in there that morning," Mitch said, furrowing his brow. "A flash of red. Maybe the guy's hat, I'm not sure."

"Was it that same guy who was kneeling over you at the accident?" Frank asked. "He was wearing a red ski cap, you said, and we found one near your watch."

Mitch bit on his lower lip. "I don't know." He stood back from the building, thinking aloud. "I went around to the alley, figuring I'd see if the back door was open."

Joe, Frank, and the sheriff followed Mitch down the alley. He approached the door that led to the inside vestibule where Frank and Joe had found the door to the basement.

"I came around to the door," Mitch said. "Yes. It's all coming back to me now. I pulled on the door handle, but just as I did, the door flew open." Mitch stumbled backward into the snow. "The guy saw me. He held out a gun. I wasn't going to be any hero—I ran for my life."

"If you touched the handle, and then backed away, that would explain why your prints were on the door, but not on the safe itself," Frank said.

"It sure would," Joe said. "Wouldn't it?" he asked Sheriff Overton.

"I should think so," the sheriff said quietly. "But I'll reserve my judgment until we get through this whole thing."

"What happened next?" Joe asked. "Can you remember?"

"It's all coming back." Mitch's voice rose a note. "I hauled off down the alley. The guy was right on my tail. I jumped onto my snowmobile. The guy had one of his own, parked right at the end of the alley, out of sight of the street."

"So the guy chased you?" Frank said.

"You bet he did." Mitch nodded emphatically. "All the way home, until I crashed."

Joe checked his watch. "We shouldn't stand around discussing this," he said. "I've got five fifty-eight. Let's head on out to the spot where Mitch crashed, and check the time once we get there."

Mitch raced back down the alley. Joe was on his heels, and Frank and the sheriff were right behind them. A minute later the foursome crossed Main Street on their snowmobiles and soon were heading down First Street to the fire road out of town.

Joe checked his watch the whole way as Mitch drove. Once he allowed for the time they'd spent talking in the alley, Joe realized that Mitch would have to have left the bank before six. But the alarm had sounded at two minutes after six, according to the sheriff. So how could Justin have seen Mitch leaving the bank *after* the alarm sounded? It was impossible to reach the crash site in three minutes. Unless . . .

At five minutes after six on the dot, Mitch pulled to a stop at the spot where he'd crashed. As soon as Frank and the sheriff came alongside, Joe shared his thoughts with his brother.

"Even allowing for the time we stood around and talked," Joe told Frank, "we still left the bank just before six, and we got here in almost exactly five minutes."

"I think I know what you're getting at," Frank said slowly. "The alarm didn't go off until six oh two. But Justin said he saw Mitch leaving the bank right after the alarm sounded."

"That means someone is lying about what happened," Sheriff Overton pointed out. "And it's either Mitch here—"

Joe finished for him. "Or someone by the name of Justin Greeley."

13 Mitch Goes Free

Joe's words hung in the air between the group. Finally, Frank broke the silence by saying, "I thought it was strange when Justin suggested that Mitch could have left work early. Remember, Joe?"

Joe knew exactly what his brother was talking about. "When we were hiking back from Secret Valley last night," he said. "What made him think Mitch left early—"

"Unless he figured out that must have been why Mitch was there?" Frank put in.

"Exactly," Joe said. He felt his excitement rising. "I think Justin Greeley has some serious questions to answer."

"You think he robbed the Evergreen Trust Company and set me up?" Mitch asked, perplexed.

"We won't know until we ask," Joe said. His mind was churning, and he began to test aloud all the various possibilities. "He could be working with George or even Rubel. We still don't know if Rob's story about his grandfather is going to wash."

"And we don't know if Justin was in on the robbery all along, or if he was an accomplice after the fact," Frank added. "Or if he just made a mistake and has an explanation for why he didn't remember the facts the way they happened."

"Whoa—" Sheriff Overton put his hands up to stop Frank. "You kids want to explain all that gobbledygook you said just now?"

Frank and Joe quickly ran down for the sheriff where they stood on their investigation. They told him about finding the money in DuPuy's safe the night before, and Rubel's explanation for how he came by his cash. Slowly, the sheriff's confused expression changed to one of amusement and then chagrin.

"So this whole time, while I was trying to put Mitch away, you boys were out there working really hard to prove me wrong," Overton said.

"You knew we were," Frank said. "You just didn't believe we'd be able to."

Overton laughed, a loud grunt in the otherwise quiet woods. "You're right, boys. That's it exactly." Then his face grew serious. "Okay. Now it's my turn. I'm going to bring Justin in, and I don't want you getting in my way. First, we'll take Mitch back and see about getting him released officially. Then I'll head over to Mount Summit Ski Rentals and talk to Justin."

Joe bristled under the sheriff's orders. He and Frank had done all the work. Now Overton wanted the credit. Frank stepped between Joe and the sheriff and brought his boot down on Joe's foot. Then he shoved Joe a few steps away from the sheriff and Mitch.

"Ouch!" Joe said, making a face. "What did you have to go and do that for?"

"Because I could see the steam coming out of your ears," Frank said, his voice low. "Chill out. We'll let Overton think he's taking it from here. But we'll know otherwise. Just play along."

Joe smiled at his brother, then nodded to the sheriff. "No problem. We'll check out the Rubel angle and track down George. But you'll let us know if you need any more of our help, right?"

"You bet," Overton said. "Come on, Mitch. Let's see about getting your stuff and collecting your 'get out of jail free' card. Looks like you earned it."

For the first time in days, Mitch shot the Hardys a broad smile. "You can't keep an innocent man in jail, Hank. Haven't I been telling you that all along?"

Forty-five minutes later Frank and Joe stood in front of the café on Main Street. Hank Overton and Mitch Taylor were still in the sheriff's station, working out the details of Mitch's release. Frank and Joe had stopped in at the café to eat a second breakfast. There, in low tones, they had discussed the case and how to proceed. Both Hardys agreed that the best lead at this point was Justin Greeley. And both agreed they weren't too keen on the idea of Overton getting to Justin first.

"Let's head over to Mount Summit Ski Rentals before he's got a chance," Joe said to Frank.

They were just crossing Main Street when Joe heard his name called out.

"Joe! Frank!"

It was Hot Doggy Dog. The snowboarder was dressed in his bright blue jacket, and he was carrying his long snowboarding backpack. He came running across the street and gave each Hardy a cheerful hello.

"Guess what I've got?" Tom asked. He shifted his pack around and drew out two motor-and-wheel contraptions. "They're for you," he said, handing them over to Frank and Joe. "My dad already had the parts. He put them together last night."

"Awesome!" Joe exclaimed, taking the contraption from Tom. "I can just slip my regular board in here, right?" he asked, pointing to the runners that ran above the motor.

"You got it," Tom told him. "It'll work on almost any board. Now you have your own original Hot Doggy Dog Catcher." Tom folded his arms across his chest. "Also, my dad said that Rubel's story

126

about his grandfather is true. He checked it out. Rob inherited ten thousand dollars, just a month ago."

Joe let out a long sigh. "So we can be pretty sure that bill we're having Heather trace won't come from the money stolen from the bank."

"There's one suspect shot down," Frank agreed.

"There's still George," Joe said. "We should head up to DuPuy Lumber and ask him a few questions."

Tom's eyes moved back and forth between Frank and Joe. "You guys are thinking pretty fast for being up so early. What gives?"

Joe explained to Tom about how they'd reenacted the robbery that morning.

"Wow," Tom said. "Did you learn anything?"

"We sure did," Frank said. "We learned that Justin Greeley may have fabricated his story. We're about to head on over to the rental shop to question him.

Puzzled, Tom bit his lower lip. "Why do you think he made up what he saw?"

Joe went over what they'd learned about the timing of the alarm and Mitch's accident. "Mitch couldn't have left the bank after six oh two, when the alarm went off."

"Maybe Justin just didn't remember right," Tom suggested, raising his eyebrows hopefully.

"Maybe." Frank looked down the street in the direction of the rental shop. "Or maybe he's lying.

There's only one way to find out, and that's to ask him."

"Well, you're gonna have to head out to Secret Valley if you want to talk to Justin," Tom said. "I was just at the rental shop looking for him. Len's there, but Justin isn't, and the copter's gone."

"Does Len think Justin took the helicopter?" Joe asked.

"I guess. He said the copter was gone when he got to work at six-thirty." Tom's gaze moved from Joe to Frank. "You guys look worried."

Joe tried to shake off the feeling coming over him. If Justin took the helicopter, he could be long gone. "What makes you think he's out at Secret Valley?" he asked Tom.

"Where else would he be?" Tom asked.

Frank and Joe exchanged a look. Both Hardys knew that if Justin had taken off, he could be anywhere. "It's worth a look," Frank said. "We've got these motors. We can rent some boards from Len and be out in Secret Valley in no time."

"Solid," Tom said. "I'm with you."

Frank and Joe headed over to Mount Summit Ski Rentals to get some snowboards. Len didn't seem happy at all when he told them about how he'd arrived at work to discover the helicopter gone.

"Justin knows how to pilot it. I'm not worried about his safety," the man said. "I just don't know why he'd take it out without my permission."

"We're going to look for him," Joe told the man.

128

"If we find him, you can be sure we'll have him fly the copter back."

From the snowfall the night before, the trail out to Secret Valley was tough going on the motorized snowboards. More than once, Frank, Joe, and Tom had to get off their boards and hike through knee-high snowdrifts. Icicles clung to branches on either side of them, and the air stayed cold, even once the sun was up.

When they got to the top of the canyon trail, Joe spotted a helicopter in the valley below. It was parked next to the snowboarder's cabin.

"There's the answer to our first question," Joe said. "We know where Justin is."

A plume of smoke rose up from the cabin. Tom slid his board out of its wheels and motor. He put the contraption, along with Frank and Joe's, into his backpack. Then he prepared to blast off the mountain. Joe yanked on Tom's coat, holding him back. "Not so fast," he said. "We need a plan."

Frank agreed. "If Justin's alone, we'll be able to get him to answer our questions. But if he's not—"

"You guys are acting like he's guilty or something," Tom snapped. "He's my friend, and I'm telling you there's an explanation for why his story doesn't match what you think happened."

With that, Tom shoved off the trail and barreled down the mountain in a spray of fresh powder. With a long sigh, Joe Hardy watched him carve up the crisp, clean slope.

"I guess we go in firing," he said to Frank.

"Tom's pretty much guaranteed that," Frank said. "Ready?"

Joe nodded. "When we get down there, I'll hang back. You can go in through the front and help Tom in case he's gotten into trouble."

"Who else do you think we'll find down there?" Frank asked.

"We're about to find out," Joe said.

Joe gave Frank a good ten minutes to get down the mountain and hike across the valley. Then he took the slope, cutting left across the mountain so he'd come down on the back side of the cabin.

The ride down was awesome. If Joe hadn't been so worried about what he was heading into, he would have enjoyed the trip more. As it was, he kept his eyes peeled on the cabin. He saw Frank enter, and then the place fell quiet again. There was no sign of a disturbance, but Joe knew better than to assume all was well.

Once Joe got to the bottom of the mountain, he worried mostly about getting some cover from the trees and boulders that dotted the valley. Using the trees, he slowly approached the cabin from the back. The copter was parked off to the side, and twice he saw Justin come out of the shack, head over to the copter, check something, and then head back inside again. Nothing seemed particularly wrong with the situation, except for the feeling Joe had in the pit of his stomach.

Keeping low, Joe crept closer. There was a stack of wood a distance from the shack that gave him his last bit of cover. After that, he'd be on open ground. If anyone looked out the back of the cabin, Joe would be spotted in an instant.

Joe drew in a deep breath. He had to get closer to the cabin to know if Frank was in trouble or not.

"Here goes nothing," he whispered to himself.

He stepped around the side of the woodpile. And found himself staring straight at Bill Forman and the barrel of a hunting rifle.

14 The Ride of Their Lives

"Nice to see you Joe," Forman said. "Join the party." Bill leveled his rifle at Joe. "We were all wondering when you'd show up," he said. "Frank and Tom are inside, waiting for you."

"Great." Joe swallowed the lump in his throat and quickly tried to come up with a plan. He could make a run for it, hike back up the mountain, and get Overton. But with Bill training a rifle on him, Joe doubted he'd get very far.

Forman seemed to realize Joe was contemplating an escape. He lunged for Joe's jacket and held him tightly by the collar.

"You won't make it," Bill said to Joe. "So don't even think about it. Let's go inside and say hello to Tom and Frank."

"So you and Justin were the ones who robbed the Evergreen Trust Company," Joe said, putting the pieces together. "You flipped the circuit breaker so the alarm wouldn't go off. How'd you manage to frame Mitch?"

Bill yanked Joe ahead of him, pushing him around the side of the shack and toward the front door. "Shut up!" he ordered. "I'm not interested in making sure all your theories line up. If you're so smart, you can figure it out on your own," Bill sneered. "You and that genius brother of yours," he added.·

Joe held back his anger. Now wasn't the time to lose his cool. "As soon as I get the upper hand over you, Forman, you'll start telling the truth."

"Fat chance," Bill said.

Holding on to Joe with one hand and his rifle with the other, Bill kicked open the door. Inside, the cabin was dark, except for the light from a fire going in the stone fireplace on the far right wall. Frank and Tom were each tied to a straight-backed chair. Justin stood over them.

"What's the plan?" Justin asked Bill, once he'd tied up Joe to a third chair. "We can't just leave these guys here."

"Sure we can," Bill said. "We'll be history by the time someone comes to help them."

"And then what?" Joe asked. "Overton is sure to find you in that copter. You won't get away."

"Sure we will," Bill told him. "In fact, we'd be

long gone if it hadn't been for that storm the night after the robbery. We'll land the copter in the woods outside Banff, then head in on our motorized snowboards. After that, there's at least three trains leaving Banff every day. We'll be on one of them, but I guess you'll have to figure out which one."

"Why didn't you leave before now?" Frank asked.

Bill scowled. "Len always had the copter out, and when he didn't, the weather was bad."

"Plus you guys were snooping around." Justin kept one eye on the boys while he went to a closet to retrieve a pack. He turned to look directly at Frank and Joe. "We thought if we stuck around, either Mitch would be arrested, or we'd be able to put you way off track."

"Then you found out about the shared electricity between the condos and the bank," Bill said. "That made things more complicated."

"That was you last night at the lumberyard," Joe said, knowing instinctively that he was right.

Bill's lips curved into a small smile. "For someone so smart, Joe, how'd you end up in a fix so dumb?"

Joe bristled, but Frank shot his brother a look. "Just for my sake," Frank said, "tell me if this is how it all happened. Bill broke into the bank, after first throwing the switch so the alarm wouldn't go off. Then Mitch came across you. You didn't expect any witnesses. You'd planned to rob the bank early enough that no one would be around. You even knew when Mitch got off work."

Justin flinched. "I guess I did let that slip, huh? Bill almost took me out over that one."

"I still wish I could figure out what triggered the alarm," Bill said. "That hadn't been part of the plan."

"Justin acted as the witness, and he lied about when he saw Mitch leaving the bank," Joe said, taking up where Frank left off. "Luckily for you, Mitch's prints were on the back door of the bank, so Overton was ready to believe he was guilty. It was your word against Mitch's."

"So?" Bill asked with a shrug. "Overton wouldn't have had enough evidence to take Mitch to trial. We knew that."

"But you were willing to risk it," Joe said.

"He messed things up," Bill said. "We had a plan, and it was working fine—until Mitch had to go and leave work early."

"Mitch found you, you got scared, so you chased him, and when he crashed his snowmobile you used the opportunity to hide five thousand dollars of the loot in his snowmobile." Frank paused. "Right so far?"

Bill and Justin exchanged a look, but neither said anything.

"I think you are," Joe told his brother. "And I think these guys never counted on Mitch to lose his memory. They planned to be long gone by that point. But once he did, they took advantage of the time it gave them."

"Gosh." Hot Doggy Dog cleared his throat, speaking up for the first time. "I trusted you guys . . . I thought you were my friends. Now I find out you're total creeps. Why'd you do it?"

Justin gave Tom an incredulous look. "Use your imagination, kid. We saw a chance and we took it. What's the big mystery? Do you think we wanted to be Evergreen bums our whole lives? No way, José."

"You didn't have to go so far," Tom said. He bent his head and rubbed his runny nose on the shoulder of his blue jacket. Joe could see he was trying to hide that he was upset. Bill and Justin had been his friends, and it couldn't be easy to find out that they were crooks. "Mitch could have gone to jail," Tom reminded them.

"Taylor's a loser," Bill said. "That's what happens to losers—they lose."

"There's one more thing," Frank said. "That was money from the robbery that you hid in George's safe last night?"

"Bingo," Bill said. "I went back and got it after I scared you two off, and now it's safe in my backpack. So if that takes care of all the details, Justin and I are going to say a quick *hasta luego* and beat it. Come on, Justin."

Justin grabbed his pack and opened the cabin door. Still pointing the rifle at the Hardys, Bill collected two sets of motors and wheels from the floor of the cabin. "Tell your dad thanks for making these," he said to Tom. "We couldn't get away without 'em."

Joe watched in frustration as Justin and Bill headed out of the cabin. Soon afterward he heard the sound of Justin firing up the helicopter.

"They're getting away," Joe said. "And we can't do a thing to stop them."

"That's where you're wrong," Frank said. He was struggling behind his back with the ropes that tied him to the chair. "I left some slack in this rope when Justin tied the knot. I think I can get out of it. Tom, can you help?"

"How?" Tom asked.

"See if you can swing your chair around behind me," Frank said, still wrestling with the knots. "Maybe you can help me undo the rope."

Even though his hands and feet were tied to the chair, Tom was able to hop the seat around until his back was to Frank. Outside, Joe heard Bill and Justin calling to each other, then the sound of the copter's engine as Justin revved it higher.

"Hurry," Joe said. "There's hardly any time. Once they get away, we'll lose them."

"Got it!" Tom announced.

Frank pulled his hands free, then quickly untied his feet. He came around and got Joe and Tom out of their ropes, too. The Hardys were just about to race out of the cabin, when Tom handed them his backpack.

137

"There are two boards in here, and two motors and wheels," he said. "Good luck!"

"Thanks," Joe said. "Come on!" he urged his brother.

The Hardys raced from the cabin just in time to see Bill boarding the copter. As soon as he saw them, Bill pointed in their direction and yelled something at Justin. The copter was only ten yards or so away. Joe made a run for it.

"What are you doing?" Frank cried. "They're taking off."

"Not without me!" Joe announced.

He ran toward the copter with Frank right behind him. Bill fired his rifle at Joe but missed. In the last second before Justin lifted off, Joe and Frank lunged for the rails.

A moment later, Justin pulled the craft up into the sky with Frank and Joe dangling below, about to have the ride of their lives.

15 One Unhappy Camper

"Can you make it?" Frank called out to his brother. "Do you have a strong grip?"

"I'd better," Joe shouted back. "Or else I'm done for."

Frank Hardy watched as the ground below fell away. He hooked his elbow through the rail, and held on—tight—as the ground receded. The cabin shrank in size and finally disappeared from view altogether.

The frigid air stiffened Frank's muscles, and his arm felt as if it were going to rip out of its socket. He wasn't sure how much longer he could hold on. But the only alternative was to let go. Frank hauled his legs up and hooked them over the rail. Joe saw what his brother was doing and did the same.

"We can't hang on like this forever," Joe shouted to Frank above the roar of the helicopter.

"I know it," Frank said. "We could use a plan. Got anything in mind?"

Below them, the valley swooped away. As Justin flew higher, they came closer to Squaw Peak. The only thing in the Hardys' favor was that now that they were underneath the copter, Bill no longer had a clear shot at them.

Frank held on, but the movement from the copter threatened to dislodge him. For several awful minutes, Frank saw the treetops getting closer and closer.

"He's trying to shake us loose," Frank cried.

"Well, it isn't going to work," Joe replied.

The copter's rails brushed the treetops. Frank felt the craft swoop upward and saw the mountainside closing in on them. They had climbed up beyond the treeline, to where the mountain was made of craggy rock covered in frozen snow. "Look out!" he warned Joe.

Justin flew the copter so close to Squaw Peak that Frank could have touched the snow if he reached out his hand. But Frank knew Justin couldn't fly so close that he'd actually dump them without also risking a crash.

Justin peeled away from the mountainside and

cut back into the valley. He risked more reckless moves, still trying to shake Frank and Joe. Every once in a while, Frank spotted Justin peering down at them through the glass side of the copter, a nasty, frustrated expression on his face.

"I don't think I can make it all the way to Banff like this," Joe said through gritted teeth. "How about you?"

"I don't even want to think about it," Frank said.

Justin flew another several hundred yards down into the valley. Frank wondered what he had planned next. Was he going to fly them straight into the mountain range across the valley, or did he have something else in mind?

They were almost to the bottom of the valley by now. As they flew back over the cabin, Hot Doggy Dog stood outside and waved them on.

"There's one person who thinks we can do it," Frank said.

Suddenly the copter took a sharp nosedive. Frank felt himself lurching forward. Joe came sliding down the rail toward him.

"What's happening?" Joe asked.

The craft shot down fast. By now they were no more than fifty feet from the valley floor, and getting closer by the second.

"They're bailing out!" Frank shouted, spotting Bill as he jumped from the craft. "Justin's crashing the copter!"

141

"Hurry," Joe urged. "Drop. Now!"

Frank didn't need any encouragement. He saw Justin jump. In another second, the copter would be crashing onto the valley floor, and he and Joe would be gone for sure. He let go and readied himself for the fall.

Frank's feet met the ground with a bone-jarring thud. Joe fell into the snow beside him. Behind them, the copter slammed into the ground, skidded a hundred yards or so, and crashed up on its side.

"That was close," Frank said, trying not to think about what might have happened.

"Too close," Joe agreed.

The Hardys picked themselves up quickly and looked around for Bill and Justin. Frank spotted Bill, already on board his motorized snowboard, dashing east across the valley.

Justin, meanwhile, was lying in the snow holding on to his leg, crying out in pain. Frank and Joe hustled back to him to discover that Justin was completely immobilized.

"I think I broke my leg when I jumped from the copter," he said. Justin gave Frank and Joe an imploring look from behind his orange-shaded sunglasses. "Help me, would you?"

Frank paused a moment. They were a good distance from the cabin. Joe indicated the crashed copter.

"I'll call Overton on the radio," Joe said. "You go after Bill."

Frank nodded. He pulled out the motor-and-wheel contraption and a snowboard from his pack. He left the spare board and motor for Joe.

"Once you get through to Overton, come out and help me," Frank said to Joe. "I have a feeling I'll need it."

"No problem," Joe said. He was already on his way to the copter. "Go get him!"

Frank slid the board into the motor and wheel and pulled the starter cord. He hopped onto the snowboard, zooming across the valley after Bill.

Bill had a good lead, but Frank was able to cut it in half pretty quickly. When Forman heard the sound of Frank's motor behind him, he tried to put on the speed, but he was already pushing his own board as hard as it could go.

Behind him, Frank became aware of the steady whine of Joe's motor, coming up fast.

"Two against one, Forman," Frank called out. "You'll never make it."

"Watch me!" Forman cried.

With that, Bill cut a wide turn to the left, heading for the woods at the north end of the valley. Frank was rattled by the move. He lost his balance and fell off the board.

The slip gave Bill extra seconds. He made valuable use of the time by disappearing into the woods.

Frank was back on his board by the time Joe came upon him. "Overton's on his way out here," Joe told his brother. "He's going to borrow a copter from the forest service. What happened to Bill?"

"He's up in those woods," Frank told his brother. "Come on. I'm not letting him get away this time."

Frank hopped back on his board and jetted into the woods. For a brief, awful moment, Frank wasn't sure they'd be able to find Bill. The terrain was rough, and there wasn't any real path to speak of. But up ahead, in the distance, he heard the steady whine of a motor.

"That's him!" Frank shouted. "Let's do it."

He cut through the tangled brush, moving in the direction of the motor. From the sound of it, Bill wasn't very far ahead. Frank and Joe were closing in when suddenly they heard the motor cut off.

"What happened?" Frank asked.

"Maybe he's run out of gas," Joe offered.

Frank cruised on through the woods. Twenty feet later, they got their answer. The woods dead-ended at a steep gorge. Two hundred feet below, a river rushed down a boulder-strewn ravine. Bill was standing at the edge of the gorge.

"Stand back or I'll jump," Bill warned, aiming his rifle in their direction.

"It's over, Bill," Frank said. "You're not getting away this time."

"That's what you think."

Bill's eyes darted right, then left. Frank could tell the guy was desperately searching for a way out. On either side was some rough terrain. Even if Bill could cut through it on his snowboard, he'd have to find a way to cross the river at some point to make his escape good.

"Keep him distracted," Frank muttered to Joe.

"Gotcha," Joe replied. "Listen, Bill, it would be better if you turned yourself in, don't you think?" Joe said. "Maybe Overton will give you a break. You're just a kid. He's not going to treat you like a hard criminal or anything."

"Sure," Bill said, with a sneer for Joe. "Overton's gonna nail me and Justin. You can be sure of that."

While Bill talked, Frank used the chance to back off and slip into the woods on his right. He knew there wasn't much time to make his move. Bill was sure to see at any moment that Frank had disappeared. Frank pushed through the brush until he was standing parallel to Bill. Then, with a wild yell, intended to startle Bill, Frank rushed out of the woods.

"I got him!" he cried, tackling Bill.

Bill struggled in Frank's grip. His rifle went flying, and Frank vaguely heard it ricochet off the walls of the gorge, only to fall down below. For a moment, Frank had the advantage. He prepared to deliver a blow to the guy's chin, but then Bill kicked him in the stomach and Frank doubled over, just for a second. It was long enough for Bill to circle around and grab Frank in a choke hold.

"Not so fast!" Frank heard Joe cry out. A moment later Joe was on Bill's back, yanking him off Frank. "I've been wanting this opportunity all morning," Joe said. "And I'm not going to miss it."

With that, Joe delivered a roundhouse punch. He hit Bill right on target. The blow smashed into Bill's jaw, and Bill went flying backward. Then, with one last groan, he fell to the ground in a heap.

"Nice work," Frank said.

"My pleasure," Joe replied.

An hour later Sheriff Overton and Len Grossman had evacuated Justin from the valley. Bill Forman was waiting already inside the same helicopter, which was standing near the Secret Valley cabin. His wrists were in cuffs, and he had a very sullen, very troubled expression on his face.

"Now, that is one unhappy camper," Joe said. "How's Mitch doing?"

Overton folded his hands across his chest. "Taylor's thrilled. He can't wait for you boys to get back to town so he can thank you in person. By the way, I got a call from Heather Harper, at the bank. She wanted to tell me that you can return the bill you dropped off for her to check to its owner. It wasn't part of the money stolen from the bank."

"I guess we figured that one out," Frank said. "Rubel's innocent, and so is DuPuy. You've got your two suspects in that copter."

"I should have known you boys wouldn't stop until Mitch was free," Overton said. "I asked around at the condo building, after you pointed out the shared electricity with the bank. Turns out one of the tenants woke up early that morning and saw the electricity was out. She went downstairs and flipped the power back on. Then the alarm went off because the wires were clipped."

"That's something I couldn't figure out," Frank said. "Why did they bother cutting those wires if the electricity that powered the alarm was off. It doesn't seem necessary."

"You mean you *don't* have all the answers to this investigation?" the sheriff asked in mock surprise.

"Maybe he doesn't, but I do," Joe interrupted. "The burglars did that to cover themselves. If the people investigating hadn't seen the clipped wires, they would naturally think there was a power outage. And checking the circuit breakers would lead them to the condos, and eventually to Bill. Am I right?"

"Right," the sheriff said. "Bill just explained that to me. He also explained that he made his getaway with the money by going down into the basement and up into the condo side of the building. That way no one would see him leaving via the bank door."

"What about DuPuy?" Frank asked. "Did you find out how he planned to come up with the money to pay back his loan?"

Overton laughed. "George got a grant, of all things, from the government. To fund research on alternatives to clear cutting! The first fifty thousand went to paying off his debts." The sheriff paused and looked inside the copter at Bill. Turning back to the Hardys, he shook their hands and said, "Listen boys, I should thank you for everything you've done."

"No problem," Joe said. "Believe me: We had a great vacation."

"Cool," Tom said. "So what are you guys going to do now that Mitch is free, and Bill and Justin are caught?" he asked.

Frank exchanged a look with his brother. "We still have two days before our flight home. And I've gotten in enough skiing this trip. What about you, Joe?"

"I've had enough snowboarding to last me a lifetime," he said.

"I've got an idea," Tom said. "Let's go to my house and rent a movie!"

"Sounds good to me," Frank said. "What do you think, Joe?"

"As long as it isn't a crime movie, I'm into it."

"We'll make some popcorn," Tom said.

"Great," Frank said. "Let's go."

"Did I tell you we have a hot tub?" Tom asked the Hardys.

"Now, this is my idea of a hard-core vacation," Joe said.

NANCY DREW® MYSTERY STORIES By Carolyn Keene

☐	#57: THE TRIPLE HOAX	69153-8/$3.99
☐	#58: THE FLYING SAUCER MYSTERY	72320-0/$3.99
☐	#62: THE KACHINA DOLL MYSTERY	67220-7/$3.99
☐	#63: THE TWIN DILEMMA	67301-7/$3.99
☐	#67: THE SINISTER OMEN	73938-7/$3.50
☐	#68: THE ELUSIVE HEIRESS	62478-4/$3.99
☐	#70: THE BROKEN ANCHOR	74228-0/$3.50
☐	#72: THE HAUNTED CAROUSEL	66227-9/$3.99
☐	#73: ENEMY MATCH	64283-9/$3.50
☐	#76: THE ESKIMO'S SECRET	73003-7/$3.50
☐	#77: THE BLUEBEARD ROOM	66857-9/$3.50
☐	#78: THE PHANTOM OF VENICE	73422-9/$3.50
☐	#79: THE DOUBLE HORROR OF FENLEY PLACE	64387-8/$3.99
☐	#80: THE CASE OF THE DISAPPEARING DIAMONDS	64896-9/$3.99
☐	#81: MARDI GRAS MYSTERY	64961-2/$3.99
☐	#82: THE CLUE IN THE CAMERA	64962-0/$3.99
☐	#83: THE CASE OF THE VANISHING VEIL	63413-5/$3.99
☐	#84: THE JOKER'S REVENGE	63414-3/$3.99
☐	#85: THE SECRET OF SHADY GLEN	63416-X/$3.99
☐	#86: THE MYSTERY OF MISTY CANYON	63417-8/$3.99
☐	#87: THE CASE OF THE RISING STAR	66312-7/$3.99
☐	#88: THE SEARCH FOR CINDY AUSTIN	66313-5/$3.50
☐	#89: THE CASE OF THE DISAPPEARING DEEJAY	66314-3/$3.99
☐	#90: THE PUZZLE AT PINEVIEW SCHOOL	66315-1/$3.99
☐	#91: THE GIRL WHO COULDN'T REMEMBER	66316-X/$3.99
☐	#92: THE GHOST OF CRAVEN COVE	66317-8/$3.99
☐	#93: THE CASE OF THE SAFECRACKER'S SECRET	66318-6/$3.99
☐	#94: THE PICTURE-PERFECT MYSTERY	66319-4/$3.99
☐	#96: THE CASE OF THE PHOTO FINISH	69281-X/$3.99

☐	#97: THE MYSTERY AT MAGNOLIA MANSION	69282-8/$3.99
☐	#98: THE HAUNTING OF HORSE ISAND	69284-4/$3.99
☐	#99: THE SECRET AT SEVEN ROCKS	69285-2/$3.99
☐	#101: THE MYSTERY OF THE MISSING MILLIONAIRES	69287-9/$3.99
☐	#102: THE SECRET IN THE DARK	69279-8/$3.99
☐	#103: THE STRANGER IN THE SHADOWS	73049-5/$3.99
☐	#104: THE MYSTERY OF THE JADE TIGER	73050-9/$3.99
☐	#105: THE CLUE IN THE ANTIQUE TRUNK	73051-7/$3.99
☐	#107: THE LEGEND OF MINER'S CREEK	73053-3/$3.99
☐	#109: THE MYSTERY OF THE MASKED RIDER	73055-X/$3.99
☐	#110: THE NUTCRACKER BALLET MYSTERY	73056-8/$3.99
☐	#111: THE SECRET AT SOLAIRE	79297-0/$3.99
☐	#112: CRIME IN THE QUEEN'S COURT	79298-9/$3.99
☐	#113: THE SECRET LOST AT SEA	79299-7/$3.99
☐	#114: THE SEARCH FOR THE SILVER PERSIAN	79300-4/$3.99
☐	#115: THE SUSPECT IN THE SMOKE	79301-2/$3.99
☐	#116: THE CASE OF THE TWIN TEDDY BEARS	79302-0/$3.99
☐	#117: MYSTERY ON THE MENU	79303-9/$3.99
☐	#118: TROUBLE AT LAKE TAHOE	79304-7/$3.99
☐	#119: THE MYSTERY OF THE MISSING MASCOT	87202-8/$3.99
☐	#120: THE CASE OF THE FLOATING CRIME	87203-6/$3.99
☐	#121: THE FORTUNE-TELLER'S SECRET	87204-4/$3.99
☐	#122: THE MESSAGE IN THE HAUNTED MANSION	87205-2/$3.99
☐	#123: THE CLUE ON THE SILVER SCREEN	87206-0/$3.99
☐	#124: THE SECRET OF THE SCARLET HAND	87207-9/$3.99
☐	#125: THE TEEN MODEL MYSTERY	87208-7/$3.99
☐	#126: THE RIDDLE IN THE RARE BOOK	87209-5/$3.99
☐	#127: THE CASE OF THE DANGEROUS SOLUTION	50500-9/$3.99
☐	NANCY DREW GHOST STORIES - #1	69132-5/$3.99

Simon & Schuster, Mail Order Dept. HB5, 200 Old Tappan Rd., Old Tappan, N.J. 07675
Please send me copies of the books checked. Please add appropriate local sales tax.

☐ Enclosed full amount per copy with this coupon (Send check or money order only)
☐ If order is $10.00 or more, you may charge to one of the following accounts: ☐ Mastercard ☐ Visa
Please be sure to include proper postage and handling: 0.95 for first copy; 0.50 for each additional copy ordered.

Name _____

Address _____

City _____ State/Zip _____

Credit Card # _____ Exp.Date _____

Signature _____

Books listed are also available at your bookstore. Prices are subject to change without notice. 760-17

THE HARDY BOYS® SERIES By Franklin W. Dixon